MW00436710

AWFUL ADVENT

AWFUL ADVENT

Karl Fieldhouse

Karl Fieldhouse

To Karen Ward,

May all your mysteries
be easily solved and
none of your Advents
be awful.

AVALON BOOKS
NEW YORK

PRINTED IN THE UNITED STATES OF AMERICA
ON ACID-FREE PAPER
BY HADDON CRAFTSMEN, BLOOMSBURG, PENNSYLVANIA

To Ruth, forever

Acknowledgements

Without the support of the Hobnail Boot Gang, this novel would still sit in unfinished form on my computer.
Thanks, Elizabeth, Ginny, and Natalie.
Inspiration constantly came (and still comes) from Steve, Maddie, and Gretchen.
I am indebted to Susan McCarty of Avalon Books, whose editorial suggestions made a good story better.

Chapter One

W└┘hen I found the body on the sacristy floor that first Sunday in December, I knew we faced an awful Advent. The blue cloths that belonged on the altar, pulpit, and lectern lay heaped around the head of the motionless figure.

Could she have fainted or collapsed while preparing the chancel for the new season? Unlikely. How would the paraments have ended up over her face? No, someone else had placed them there. My peaceful little sacristy had mutated into a murder scene.

My hand shook as I knelt by the body and felt for a pulse. No luck. I looked at my watch. An hour before Sunday School, more than two hours before the church service. Could I cancel the whole morning? No, Alvin would have a fit. Maybe the emergency services would clear the sacristy in time for everything to come off on schedule.

And maybe the saints in the stained glass windows of St. Luke's Church would jump down from their places and dress the altar, put out the vessels for Holy Communion, and clean up the sacristy.

At last the identity of the person on the floor registered in my confused and racing brain. Nancy Huff, the president of the altar guild. I'd know those tan penny loafers and blood-red, three-inch-long fingernails anywhere.

Shaking more from the presence of a peculiar death (as a pastor, I took normal death in stride) than the cold of the

1

drafty old building, I backed into the nave of the church and leaned against the door frame. The phone. I had to get to my office and call 911.

Then I noticed the processional cross under the sacristy window, about four feet from Nancy's body. I stared dumbly at its empty stand by the door, then back at the cross. No, I hadn't imagined it. Dark streaks of blood and a few strands of hair stood out against the gold surface. My stomach flipped, threatening to empty itself. The ridiculous thought crossed my mind that I'd have to justify violating the crime scene.

Yes, the sacristy of St. Luke's Church had become a crime scene, soon to be decked in yellow tape. Preparing for Christmas normally had congregational life in an uproar. This would magnify every little problem, for pastor as well as for congregation. I sighed as I imagined what Alvin Porter, the board president, would say. It wouldn't be good, and it would be aimed directly at me, his anything-but-favorite clergyperson.

I ran like the track star I'd never been across the chancel and down the hall into the education wing. After three tries, I finally slipped the trembling key into the lock, turned it, and entered the church office. I grabbed the phone and dialed. Afterwards I couldn't recall what I'd said, but I must have gotten the essentials across, because the ambulance arrived just as the board vice president, Barb Johnson, pulled into the parking lot.

Barb had the build of an NFL fullback, and her bright red beehive enhanced her already considerable height.

"I heard the call on my scanner." Huffing loudly from running into the building, her arms loaded with Sunday School materials and robes freshly pressed for the children's choir, Barb collapsed into my desk chair.

"Come with me to the back doors," I said. "I have to let the emergency technicians in."

"What's happened?" For a large person, she kept up with me effortlessly on our quick journey to the rear of the hall.

"I found a body on the sacristy floor when I got here a little bit ago."

Her red eyebrows, a shade or two darker than her beehive, reached for her hairline. "Anyone we know?"

"I'm afraid so. Nancy Huff."

"Nancy Huff? You can't mean it."

"I wish I didn't, but I'm pretty sure it's Nancy."

Barb's face scrunched up. "Messy, huh? I don't blame you for not turning her over. What do you think? Heart attack?"

I placed one hand on her arm and pulled the door open for the EMTs with the other. "Nothing that easy, if I'm guessing right. She's on her back, but I can't tell for certain if it's Nancy."

"Why not?"

"Hey, lady," the younger EMT said, "you going to stand here and talk all morning, or you going to take us to the person who's collapsed?"

"You'll see," I told Barb as I motioned for the men to follow me toward the nave of the church.

"Deader than road kill," the younger EMT judged, earning himself a look of rebuke from his partner. "We can't even step into the room until the cops get here. You all know her?"

Barb and I looked at each other. Neither of us responded.

"Hey, ladies, it's not a difficult question. You know her or you don't. Which is it?"

Barb propped her hands on her hips and leaned closer to him. "Has it occurred to you, young man, that our day has gotten off to a horrible start and doesn't promise to get any better real soon? Yes, we know her. Nancy Huff's belonged to St. Luke's longer than I can remember. Her death will be a blow to this church. It's sure as shooting a blow to the pastor here and me, and we could do without your rudeness."

He had the grace to blush and mutter an apology.

"I suppose one of us had better call Alvin," I said. "Do you think there's any chance we can have a normal Sunday School hour?" Normal would be good, as my intestines kept signaling me.

"Doubt it." Barb shook her red beehive. "The kids would all be back in the education wing, but that adult class meets out here. Knowing some of them, they'd have their noses stuck so far into this sacristy the police wouldn't be able to squeeze past without a shoehorn."

"The police will investigate this, won't they?" She directed this at the older EMT, who looked as if he'd actually been out of high school for more than two years. Possibly as many as four. From my lofty position of nine years past high school and a whole year and a half since seminary and my ordination, I felt immensely more mature than these youngsters.

"Yes, ma'am," he answered. "You can bet the church's morning offering on a long, thorough investigation. Somebody gave this woman a quick shove into eternity."

When I thought of facing Alvin, I didn't feel a single day older than the EMTs. As I glanced down at Nancy's body, I noticed I had somehow torn a hole on the right shin of my pantyhose.

Drat, rats, and cootie juice.

Could I possibly find time to rush home and change? It didn't matter. I felt sure this was my last intact pair. From my queasiness, I judged my innards to be no better off.

"You're as white as the fair linen. Maybe you should sit down. Do you want me to go call Alvin?" Barb said. Sometimes I think she can read my mind, which is not entirely good. If she can figure out what I'm thinking, maybe Alvin can, too.

As if he ever gets as far out of himself as the skull of

the next person in the room. A pastor should be more generous, I'm sure, in assessing her parishioners. On the other hand, the truth is the truth.

"Yes, call him. He has to know sooner or later," I said.

I whirled around at the sound of footsteps and almost ran smack into the most gorgeous hunk of cop I'd ever seen. He stood about a foot taller than I, with a sprinkling of freckles across his nose and short blond hair cut in typical cop style. At the angle he held his notepad, his biceps had the arms of his state police uniform shirt stretched tight. I caught myself unconsciously hooking a strand of my mousy brown hair over my right ear.

What had happened to my mind? I'd just found the dead body of a parishioner in the church, and I needed to check the front of my dress to make sure I hadn't drooled down it? Hunk or not, this officer came to investigate a suspicious death, not to check out the available young women.

"Pull in your tongue," Barb whispered in my ear.

Either the officer heard her or guessed she'd said something about him from her expression or mine, because he blushed an appealing shade of red. Those freckles disappeared momentarily.

"Ladies," he said, "I realize this has been a shock, but I need to get a lab team out here. Not much question of the cause of death. Has the crime scene been disturbed?"

When I'd explained everything I'd done and touched, the cop seemed relieved. "Could we go somewhere else so I can ask you both some questions?"

My fears came to life when Officer Hunk ran a strip of yellow tape across the door of the sacristy, just where worshipers in the front pews could see it. I wondered where the EMTs had gotten to. I assumed they would still remove Nancy's body once the lab team had completed their work. Maybe not. Maybe the coroner would have to examine the body and then take it away. Though I thought I had a degree of sophistication about death, I hadn't the slightest idea how authorities handled a suspicious death.

Suspicious death? Who was I kidding? A murder.

For the next twenty minutes, Barb and I told Officer E. Eichelberger (I finally read the nametag pinned to his shirt) about finding the body, the church's security system (virtually nonexistent), and a little about Nancy Huff. He took our names and phone numbers, told me in particular he'd be in touch, and headed back to the body.

As soon as Officer Eichelberger's uniform disappeared through the office doorway, Alvin Porter rushed in, nearly foaming at the mouth. "Well, I suppose you want to cancel the church service."

"Why don't we ask the lab people how long their work will take once they get here?" I suggested, forcing myself to smile.

Alvin hadn't heard a word I'd said. "If we do cancel, you know, we'll lose a whole week's offering. Bad for the budget, very bad. You don't have the experience yet to realize this, but churches depend on the giving at the end of the year. Our receipts run behind the budget well into the summer. With tax concerns pushing them, members open those wallets in December and rack up the deductions."

He looked out the window, frowned at the presence of the state police vehicles, and spun around to face me. "A body in the sacristy. Bad publicity for St. Luke's. Never had to put up with anything like this before." The look he gave me allowed no-misunderstanding about whom he held responsible for this sorry state of affairs.

Barb yanked the sleeve of his navy polyester blazer. "Chill out, Alvin. If you have a stroke, the ambulance will have to transport you to the hospital in Frederick along with Nancy's body."

Even pulled to his full height, Alvin still stood a good four or five inches shorter than Barb. He glared up at her as if she'd spit on his shiny wingtips. "Hardly a moment to play the comedian, Barb. As vice president of the board, you should know better."

Barb sighed. "You're right. I shouldn't joke at a tragedy like this."

Alvin removed his glasses and wiped them with his tie, an engaging piece of haberdashery featuring a dancing troupe of elk. "I'm glad you see it my way. The loss of a Sunday's revenue would be a severe blow to this church. We face enough problems already." He replaced the glasses and gave me a fish-eyed stare.

"Lost revenue?" I blurted. "Wouldn't you consider Nancy's death more of a tragedy than losing today's offering? Think how her family will feel. After all, you just told me people contribute more near the end of the year, so recouping it shouldn't be impossible."

He shifted the knot of his tie deeper into the folds of his bull neck. "Not everyone will agree Nancy's death counts as a loss to this church, you know. She may have had her fingers in a lot of pies, but no one would ever mistake her for our most popular member. Only became president of the altar guild because no one else wanted the job. With her on the guild, you have to wonder how we managed to keep anyone else on it."

By this time a line of Sunday School teachers rivaling the crowds waiting to buy season tickets for the Baltimore Orioles had backed up in the hallway.

"Pastor, is it true there's a dead body in the sacristy?" the children's superintendent asked. "We've heard Nancy Huff died. Should we go ahead with our lessons?"

"Yep, she bought the farm," Alvin confirmed.

If I had laser vision, Alvin Porter would have turned into a big grease spot on my desk blotter at that moment. For once he got the message and clamped his jaw shut.

"We might as well keep to the schedule," I said. "I think we'll have to move the service to the fellowship hall, and the kids will act a little scattered if they've heard about the body, so don't tell them if they don't know. And by all means keep them in the education wing."

"We'll get through this," Barb assured the waiting mob of anxious teachers. She shooed them down the hall with repeated waves of her muscular arms, and most of them went off whispering in tight groups.

But the superintendent persisted. "What do we say if the kids already know?"

"Tell them we don't know what's happened, because we don't." I snapped the plastic insert out of my clerical collar and turned it over in my hand. "Tell them they can ask their parents about it when they get home."

With a vigorous nod, the superintendent went off to marshal her troops.

"Nice move, Pastor Abby." Alvin's paw descended toward my shoulder, and I barely managed to avoid it by dropping the collar insert and bending over to retrieve it from the floor. "You may have the makings of a real pastor yet. Stroke of genius, putting the service in the fellowship hall. With luck, the TV and radio stations will pick this up any minute. Why, people might fill up this place as if it was Christmas Eve when they hear something this exciting's going on."

Barb looked at me and rolled her eyes. For a second, I considered whether it was too late to faint.

I hate it when someone says something stupid and turns out right. We had to line up chairs in the hallway for the overflow from the fellowship hall that morning. After ascertaining the police had searched the bushes and trees around the church for any evil-intentioned lurkers, I escaped from church before they finished counting the offering and didn't have to hear Alvin crow about the biggest total of contributions since Easter. Naturally, he left a message on my answering machine at home, bringing me up to date on the monetary details and the arrival of the first TV news van. That had the advantage of allowing me to make faces at him without any danger of being caught.

After attacking an innocent cup of yogurt for lunch, I bounced my collar tab off the mirror on the dresser and collapsed on my bed, prepared to spend the next hour imagining myself in the company of bulging biceps and a cute nose dusted with freckles. But my conscience dragged me to the phone to call the Huff family and set up a time to talk to them.

How would the circumstances of Nancy's death affect the timing of the funeral? I'd never had a burial where the authorities had removed the body for an autopsy. I'd never performed a funeral for someone who'd been murdered. My heart went out to John Huff, a quiet man who'd taken Nancy's abrasiveness in apparent good humor for as many years as my parents had been married. He'd also acted as my advocate when Alvin opposed the congregation's calling me as pastor.

No answer at the Huff house, just the recorded invitation to leave my name and number for a return call. Then I remembered John always went to Pennsylvania deer hunting on this weekend. More than likely he wouldn't come home until evening and hadn't heard about his wife's death, though their son must have by now. I called that number with the same result.

I had just tossed my black skirt and clergy shirt over the nearest chair, determined to close my eyes and get back to those freckles, when the doorbell rang. I thought about ignoring it but decided I couldn't. I pulled on a pair of jeans and a sweatshirt and rushed down to the front door.

When I opened it, my neighbor Dora Knaub stood on the porch. A dear person, a real salt of the earth type, but her timing often leaves something to be desired.

"Hi, Abby. I brought you some tomatoes." She shook the small paper bag in her hand.

I motioned her in and closed the door. "Dora, you may have the greenest thumb in central Maryland, but even you can't get tomatoes to grow in your garden in December." I gave her my version of my mother's "I don't believe you" look.

Dora flashed me a victorious smile. "They're hydroponic. I've started growing them in the glassed-in porch at the back of the house. Taste a lot better than those plastic things you get at the supermarket this time of year."

She led the way to my kitchen, put them down on the counter, filled the teakettle, set it on the stove, and turned on the burner.

"Gee, can you stay long enough to have a cup of tea?" I asked.

"Save your sarcasm for your momma," Dora said. In a weak moment I'd told her about the quiet but famous battles my mother and I waged. "Well, don't just sit there. Give me the goods." She pulled her chair closer to mine and tugged her flowered apron into a more comfortable position.

"The goods?"

"You know. Nancy Huff."

I groaned.

"Oh, no, you're not getting out of it that easily. I've listened to your trials and tribulations for more than a year. Now you've got some good stuff to tell instead of that boring old church stuff, so don't figure I'm going to let you get away without filling me in on the details."

"You'd probably get more on the evening news. I'm not sure I know that much. Or that I'm allowed to tell what I do know."

"Yeah, police investigation going on and all that. Look, you know what you tell me stops with me. May a giant eagle descend and tear out my tongue if I spread one word past that door."

While not a single word I'd ever told Dora had come

back to me from another source, I hesitated. She did like a good story, in the hearing or in the telling, but she seemed to think of me as the daughter she'd never had. Our conversations had taken on a character not unlike the confidences my parishioners shared with me in my pastoral role.

"If I tell a living soul what you say about this, may a black bear come down Catoctin Mountain, break into my house, raid my refrigerator, and rip me to pieces as I lie in my bed."

I suppressed a giggle, but she knew she had me.

"Okay, girl. Start talking." She threatened me with a green checked potholder.

I recounted my morning, including the important details like Alvin's tie, my torn pantyhose, the blood and hair on the processional cross, and the huge attendance. I omitted any mention of biceps or freckles.

"Who investigated?" Since Dora had a nephew in the state police, she knew many of the officers.

"Oh, they sent out a lab team," I said casually. "I didn't get their names."

"No, no, no. What cop came out from Frederick?"

"Some young guy. Not your nephew."

"Of course not my nephew, or I'd be giving you details instead of the other way around. He had to have a name."

"The officer could have been a woman, you know," I said, brushing some imaginary crumbs off the tablecloth.

Dora knocked some of the invented crumbs from her apron. "Sure. But you already said it was some guy. Some young guy. Do I smell a smidgen of interest here?"

"What you smell is the teakettle burning dry on the stove."

Dora ran to rescue the damaged item, shot me her most disgusted look when she found it steaming but undamaged, poured the water, and brought the two cups of steeping Earl Gray to the table.

"So you thought he was cute."

"I thought he was young. Not the same thing."

"It is when you get to be my age." She stirred two teaspoons of sugar into her cup, licked the spoon, and laid it in the saucer.

"Eye—something."

"Must be a new guy. Never heard of one from the Frederick barracks whose name started with an I. Well, Ilgenfritz, but he's not there anymore, and if he's young, I'm Madonna. Try a little harder. Scratch your head. Try a *lot* harder."

"Eichel—something," I muttered.

With a whoop, Dora leaped from her chair so fast she bumped into the table and sent tea sloshing over the edges of both cups. "Eichelberger! You've got the hots for Ike Eichelberger."

In a solemn voice I usually reserve for funerals, I informed her, "I do not have the 'hots,' as you put it, for this police officer, whatever his name is. As a pastor, my calling is the care of the souls in my charge, and one of them has had her life rudely and prematurely ended."

Dora sat back down on her chair but didn't remove the smile from her face. "Yep, you're good at what you do. Those folks over at St. Luke's are lucky to have you. But you were a woman before you were a pastor, and that runs deeper, honey. You haven't told me about the warts on his chin or how far over his belt his belly hangs, so I'm betting you think he's cute."

I shrugged. "He's a pleasant-looking man, he's young, he conducted himself in a professional manner at the church, and he has no concept that I even exist. Ike? Are you sure? His nameplate gave just a first initial, E."

"If I've ever heard another name for him, and I probably did when he was born, I don't remember it. Always heard him called Ike. Family's from Thurmont. I went to school with his mother's cousins. Probably some of his father's cousins, too, come to think of it. Just pleasant-looking, huh? Weak chin? Beady eyes? Glasses like binoculars? Hooked nose?"

"Okay, okay. You win. He's a hunk."

Dora's feet did a little dance in front of her chair. "I knew it, I knew it. So, are you going to call him?"

"No. He has his job to do, I have mine. If I hear from him again, he'll want more information about Nancy or who has access to the church. Stuff like that."

The feet did a few more steps. "Beats no stuff at all."

The doorbell rang, providing me a way out of this conversation that felt like some kind of contest I couldn't win. Probably John Huff or his son, responding to my answering machine message.

When I opened the door, my breathing stopped for at least five seconds. I really had to talk to the church's property committee about getting a peephole installed. I'd justify the expense by telling them it would help prevent the pastor from having heart attacks.

E. Eichelberger stood on my porch.

Chapter Two

"May I come in, Miss Shaw?" the hunk on my porch said.

"Pas—," I rasped.

A frown scrunched the freckles together. "Miss Pass? I have your name down as Shaw."

"I mean Pastor Shaw. Never mind. Come on in." I listened for the sound of the back door closing. When I didn't hear it, I knew Dora stood just out of sight in the kitchen doorway, ready to snoop on everything we'd say.

I led the state trooper into the living room and sat down on the couch across from the chair he'd chosen. "I have a visitor you may know, Dora Knaub. She went to school with relatives of yours. Dora, come on in and say hello to Officer Eichelberger."

A few heartbeats later, Dora appeared in the archway. "Did you call me, Abby?" She straightened the bib of her apron and smiled warmly at the man in the tan leather armchair.

"I think you know Officer Eichelberger," I said.

"Not really," my neighbor replied. "Just some of his relatives."

"Nice to meet you, Mrs. Knaub." The young man stood and shook her offered hand.

"I know your cousin Albert."

"Would that be Albert B. or Albert P.?"

"Oh, Albert P., I think. They call him Petey. He and my son Norman used to run around together."

"Yeah, Petey. Actually, he's my uncle. But you've got the right family."

"Why don't you come over at suppertime and share a sandwich with me?" I asked, hinting that Dora should go home now. "We can slice those tomatoes you brought me and put them on some chicken salad."

She scratched her nose. "You've got a date, Abby. You young people have a nice talk, now."

This time the back door closed with a decisive thud.

The trooper leaned back against the chair, his skin only a shade lighter than its leather. "We can't seem to find either the victim's husband or son. Would you have any idea of the whereabouts of John or Bill Huff?"

"I know John goes north to hunt deer in Pennsylvania this weekend every year. I suppose Bill could have gone with him, but I doubt his wife, Suzie, did. I've tried to contact them too, but I only got machines."

"Oh, yeah, funeral arrangements, right?"

"When can we have the funeral? I mean, when will they release the body?"

"You can call the county coroner's office tomorrow afternoon and ask. I don't think there will be much of a delay. The basic facts seem pretty straightforward. What can you tell me about Nancy Huff?"

I glanced out the window at the bare tree limbs framing my view of the road. A lone sparrow turned its head toward me as if it knew I was watching. "She belonged to St. Luke's for many years, long before I became its pastor."

"That can't be very long ago."

"No, just eighteen months."

"But you did know her, know how people felt about her," he prodded.

"Nancy had a way of ruffling people's feathers," I admitted. "She had her defenders, but she seemed to make enemies faster than she made friends."

"So she had a lot of enemies. Who would you include in that group?"

A current of fear ran through me. I certainly didn't want to accuse anyone of murdering Nancy—or even place anyone on a list of suspects.

"I meant that as a figure of speech. She would never have won a vote as Miss Congeniality. That's all I meant. I can't think of anyone who'd have a reason to want her dead. Gagged and locked in a closet, maybe, but not dead."

Where had *that* come from? The trooper must have seen my embarrassment at the slip, because a tiny grin flashed and disappeared.

"How about her work?"

"She worked for a lawyer in Frederick as a paralegal. I don't remember his name."

"Problems there?"

"I have no idea. Look, Nancy was rough on people, but she was competent at what she did. I never thought of her as the kind of person others would lie in wait to kill."

"You think someone planned this instead of just taking advantage of an opportunity?"

Hand me a shovel and a pile of dirt, and I'll dig myself a hole and crawl in. I felt like crying. Officer Hunk had to think me scatterbrained, prevaricating, or guilty of Nancy's murder myself. I imagined how I'd look in a state-supplied jumpsuit. Could I alter one of those with a little quick sewing so I could insert a clerical collar?

"How did you get along with the victim?"

My right hand clasped my throat, checking for a noose, perhaps. "We had our ups and downs. As head of the altar guild, Nancy took charge of a number of things that affected the services at the church. I didn't always do things the way previous pastors had done them, which never failed to bother her. Nancy didn't handle change very well."

"We didn't find any sign of forced entry at the church. Did you notice anything unusual when you got there this morning?"

I closed my eyes and transported myself back to those moments right before I'd discovered Nancy's body on the sacristy floor. "The cloth hangings for Advent hadn't been put up, and that's unusual. That's always done by the time I get there on Sunday. Almost always, anyway. I thought maybe there'd been some mix-up over who had the December altar guild duty. Nothing else seemed out of order."

"Did you see anyone else, any cars driving away, perhaps, as you drove into the parking lot?" His pencil hovered over his notepad.

"No one. I saw a dark blue car at the other end of the lot from my parking space, but it didn't dawn on me that it was Nancy's until later. Sometimes a Sunday School teacher or two will beat me to church, so I didn't think anything of it. I'm afraid I didn't notice anything or anyone else."

He had me repeat what I'd told him earlier about finding the body: what I'd touched, who else had been in the room before the lab team arrived.

"Would you be willing to go out to the church and take another look around right now, just in case you notice something you didn't before?"

I grabbed my keys and followed him to the police car, wondering all the time if the neighbors would think he was taking me to jail. Not Dora. She'd think he had asked me for a date and had taken me out for a drive or to dinner. Maybe both.

Officer E. Eichelberger and I checked every entrance to the church, both outside and inside, looking unsuccessfully for anything suspicious. When we got to the sacristy, I found the paraments piled in a corner and a number of other items shoved against the wall under the window.

"I'd better straighten up this room before the altar guild decides to hang me from the Christmas tree," I said.

The cop opened a folding chair and sat down. "Tell me more about Mrs. Huff."

"I can't think of much that could help you. She and John had only one child, Bill. He's married to Suzie, whom I never see in church. Rumor has it that's so she doesn't have to spend any more time than necessary in the presence of her mother-in-law. Nancy had an artistic eye, loved to arrange flowers, and tried her hand at just about every craft you can think of. I've seen some of her needlework. Beautiful. Like everything she did, it shows an amazing attention to detail. None of this is helpful, is it?"

With a shrug and a crooked grin, he acknowledged the truth of that. "Think the daughter-in-law—Sue?"

"Suzie."

"Yeah, Suzie. Think she disliked her mother-in-law enough to give her a good bash on the head?"

I hesitated and made a quick survey of the room. Yes, the lab team had taken the processional cross. Of course they would, along with the blue paraments as evidence.

"Still considering it?" the cop hunk prodded.

"No, just taking stock of the room. Frankly, I think Suzie would consider violence too much trouble."

"You don't care for her."

"I don't dislike her." The defensive tone of my voice annoyed me. "I just recognize her—well, her disconnection from things, I guess."

"You minded her avoidance of her mother-in-law?"

I'd never see this man again once he'd completed his investigation into Nancy's death. Why should I care what he thought? But I did. Freckles do the worst things to me. I won't even mention the effect they have coupled with good biceps.

"No. It's just part of Suzie's general pattern of life. Are you thinking I'm trying to put her in a bad light?"

The crooked grin again. "You strike me as a pretty good judge of people. Not just because of your profession. Seems to me it can't hurt to know how you size up the people closest to Nancy, especially here, in the context where she died."

I turned away so he couldn't see the smile I felt breaking out on my face.

When I arrived back home, I found eight messages on my answering machine. Three members of the altar guild wanted to know when they could get into the sacristy to clean up. Considering who made those calls, I figured one meant exactly that and the other two really meant, "How soon can I snoop?"

Four members of the church called to see how I was feeling after the morning's trauma. St. Luke's had some really sweet people who helped balance the chronic complaining that, according to the stories told by the oldest members and a little reading between the lines in church documents and histories, had become as institutionalized there as the red bricks in the outer walls.

The eighth call came from Bill Huff.

His extremely brief message asked me to come to his house rather than return the call. I looked at the mantel clock and calculated whether I had time to have those sandwiches I'd promised Dora. Probably not.

Bill and Suzie lived in a semi-detached house in one of Thurmont's newer developments. That hadn't kept Bill from keeping his ties with St. Luke's, but it offered Suzie a number of alternatives to our rural fellowship. From what I'd heard, she'd tried out several of the town churches without finding a place to call home.

Someone in the block was hosting a party, so I had to drive around the development looking for a parking space. Given the twists and turns of the streets, I didn't want to park too far away because I could wander for half an hour trying to find my car after my visit. I had just about given up when the loop brought me unexpectedly back in front of Bill and Suzie's home, where a parking space had appeared.

Synchronicity, maybe. I'd say an answer to prayer, but that might be stretching it. For one thing, I'd concentrated on the possible pitfalls of making the funeral arrangements and hadn't thought or whispered anything the least bit like a prayer. Could I have experienced an example of what St. Paul meant by "pray without ceasing?" Or had one good thing finally happened today?

Suzie answered the door. From her red eyes, I could see she'd been weeping. Copiously. Had we all misjudged her relationship to her mother-in-law? Had we projected our own feelings about Nancy onto Bill's wife? She led me to the kitchen and began to make tea. Bill sat at the kitchen table, staring out the window toward Catoctin Mountain. I sat down across from him.

"I'm so sorry for your loss," I began. "Planning your mother's funeral won't be easy for any of us. Has your dad come home yet?"

Bill shifted uncomfortably in his chair. "I drove out there half an hour ago to see. He hadn't gotten back then. I called a few minutes ago, but he didn't answer. Pastor, this is going to be awful."

"Yes, Bill," I agreed. "Whenever someone as young as your mother dies, handling the grief doesn't come easy. With a sudden loss, it gets harder. Then you add the unusual circumstances, and—"

His laughter startled me. "Unusual circumstances. That's a good one, Pastor Abby. Yeah, I suppose murder is pretty unusual, at least in this part of the state."

My jaw must have dropped down, because he blushed and rubbed his hands from his hairline to his chin.

"She'd want 'Amazing Grace' sung," Suzie said. She put steaming mugs of tea in front of each of us and took the chair between her husband and me. "She loved that hymn. When my mother was dying of cancer, Nancy visited her three or four evenings a week. They'd sing together, that song most of all."

I pulled a notebook out of my purse and wrote the hymn down. "Do you know your mom's date of birth?"

Bill swallowed hard, and Suzie came to his rescue with the appropriate information.

"Have you thought about a church funeral?" I asked.

They looked at me as if I had just suggested they vacation on Mars.

"I know funerals in the church aren't as popular here as in some parts of the country, but your mom belonged to St. Luke's all her life and played such an active role there. Don't you think she would have wanted the recognition of her life conducted in the place she gave so much of her effort to?"

They shared another of those looks that pass between couples with the hope the communication remains opaque to observers.

"Oh, it's not that," Suzie said. "We thought you'd ... we expected you'd want to wait for Bill's dad before making arrangements."

"Of course," I agreed. "You don't want to suggest anything he might feel obligated to approve even if he'd prefer something different."

Another one of those telepathic messages crossed the corner of the table.

I folded my red leather notebook. As I stuck it in my purse, I pulled out the book with the occasional services and prayers. I fingered the black ribbon that marked the service for the recently bereaved.

"If you think of something you'd like in the service, call me or leave a message at the church office. Would you feel comfortable if we had a short prayer service together now?"

The instant relief on their faces surprised me so much I sat there until Suzie prompted me.

"Yes, Pastor, we'd like that very much. Go right ahead."

During the prayers and scriptures, I couldn't ignore the way Bill gripped the edge of the table or the flash of Suzie's rings as she folded and unfolded her fingers.

We talked for a few moments about Nancy's hobbies and the highlights of her life. Suzie's insight into her mother-in-law struck me again. If she hadn't liked her very much, and I was still inclined toward that opinion, she certainly knew the woman, down to her favorite colors for suits and blouses (tan and cream, respectively) and the meal she ordered most often in a restaurant (fried butterfly shrimp, Caesar salad, steamed kale, and apple pie with chocolate ice cream.)

Our conversation turned to the upcoming holidays, and my heart went out to them. What a bleak time lay ahead for them instead of a joyous holiday season.

After a while, I smiled, thanked them for their time and the tea, and headed for the door.

When we got to the living room, Bill blurted out the names of some family friends and church members he thought would gladly serve as pallbearers. I whipped out the notebook and added them below "Amazing Grace."

I buttoned up my coat and said goodbye again.

He put his hand on my elbow, then shook his head and took a step back.

"Bill," I said, "is there something more you'd like to ask me? Or tell me?"

Suzie may have thought she'd poked him in the ribs quite subtly, but I suspect the army could conduct less obvious troop movements through Times Square during rush hour.

"Pastor Abby, if I tell you something as my pastor, you can't share it with anyone, right?" Perspiration shone on Bill's upper lip.

"That's right," I said.

"Not even the police?" he added.

I nodded. A bad feeling formed in my stomach and crept quickly up into my throat.

He looked at Suzie. She mouthed, "Go on!"

"Pastor, I think . . ." He examined the carpet and scraped his shoe across it like a tennis player dragging his foot across the baseline during a serve.

He shook his head and tried again.

"I think my father murdered my mother."

Chapter Three

T hank heavens a chair sat near their door. I immediately
sank onto it and dropped my purse. "Could you repeat what
you just said?" I asked.

Bill wiped both palms on the outside of his jeans. "Yeah,
I know. Sounds all wrong, doesn't it? But that's what I
think. That my dad did it. Killed Mom."

Suzie had retreated just inside the kitchen, where she
stood biting a thumbnail and listening to every word.

I dropped my purse onto the floor beside the chair and
took several deep breaths. "I think you'd better sit down
and tell me more."

Bill did the toe-dragging act again. "I'd rather stand."

I nodded. Okay, he could stand. At the moment, I
wouldn't attempt anything so brave. My head threatened to
convince my body to dive for the rug, and my stomach had
fallen into my inner depths with a bigger thump than my
purse had made. "Why do you suspect your father?"

He looked over his shoulder at Suzie, who slipped a few
feet farther into the kitchen.

"They've both been acting funny lately. Avoiding each
other, arguing when they were together. That never happened before."

That carpet would have a channel deep enough to sail
clipper ships if he kept up the toe dragging.

24

"That doesn't sound pleasant, but I wouldn't call it grounds for murder," I suggested.

He looked over his shoulder at his wife, who managed to empty the dishwasher while passing the doorway with each plate or cup on its way to the cupboard.

"I guess what I've noticed is the atmosphere. You know what I mean? Like some sort of negative charge between them." He shrugged. "Maybe I can't explain it."

He had to be holding something back. Did he feel guilty for not preventing his mother's death? For ratting out his father, even to a pastor who couldn't repeat what he told her? Something else clouded this issue for him, but I couldn't guess what. "Has you father done anything violent? Has he said anything that made you think your mother was in danger?"

Another two millimeters of rug bit the dust.

"They had a terrible fight last week when we had them here for dinner. Dad shouted at Mom and tore out of here. Left her without a ride home. I had to take her, and she . . . well, you knew Mom. She had a few things of her own to say."

"What did he yell?"

Another layer of carpet dissolved.

"That she didn't deserve to live."

I tried to hide my surprise. "I've never heard your father make such a strong statement. He must have been extremely angry with her."

"Yeah, really out of character for Dad, wasn't it?"

I stared at him, willing him to get the message that he'd better provide some reason for all this or I was out the door.

He cleared his throat. "When I saw Dad the next day, I asked him what had made him so mad. He said . . . well, he thought Mom was messing around with someone else."

Only by the grace of God did I manage to keep from falling off my chair onto the floor. Nancy Huff? Messing around? Did Frederick County harbor anyone desperate enough to have an affair with her? I shoved the ungenerous thought away.

"Do you think he had grounds for his speculation?" The pace of dishes crossing between the dishwasher and the cupboards had picked up considerably. I wondered for a second how many trips some of them had made.

Bill shrugged and glanced quickly toward the kitchen. "Not like Dad to make accusations, really. Didn't seem like Mom to be interested in another guy, but how do I know? Maybe she got bored. They haven't had an exciting life. Dad has his hunting and fishing. Mom acted restless lately, now that I think about it. Maybe that's where Dad got the idea. I don't think there's anything else I can tell you. What do you think I should do?"

"You mean, do I think you should tell the police?"

He nodded. "Or someone."

A restless mother and an angry father. Hardly enough to put John Huff behind bars.

"Why don't you just keep your own counsel for a while?"

"Yeah. Maybe I'm wrong. I don't want to be right about this. But I can't figure out why anyone would want to hurt Mom."

Off the top of my head, I could have listed several people who would have disagreed with that assessment, so I just hummed a syllable I hoped he'd interpret as concurrence.

After a quick farewell in the direction of the kitchen, I promised Bill I'd contact him again about funeral arrangements and would see him at the viewing. He sighed with obvious relief as I walked out the door, either because he'd gotten something off his chest or because I had finally left. Or maybe because he didn't have to worry any longer about the listener in the kitchen.

No sooner had I hung my coat in the closet than the phone rang. I considered letting the answering machine screen the caller for me, but I decided not to delay bedtime any longer than necessary tonight. Earlier I hadn't thought I'd sleep for days, considering the way the picture of Nancy lying on the sacristy floor kept popping into my mind. Now I felt as if I'd taken a drug. I longed to pull the duvet over my head and stay in bed until next Saturday. Then I'd have to get up to write the next day's sermon.

That could never happen, of course. I had a funeral to do this week. And who knew what else, given the circumstances?

I made my voice as cheery as possible. "Hello, St. Luke's parsonage, Pastor Abby speaking."

"Abby, this is John Huff. I just got home from Pennsylvania a few minutes ago. You left a message to call, so I'm answering it. Is Nancy there? Or at the church? I don't see any sign she's been around today. Guess she could have gone down to Baltimore to visit her sister, but she usually leaves a note."

He didn't know. Either that or he deserved an Academy Award for best actor in a deadly drama.

"Did you get any other messages?"

"Yeah. Strange one from Bill, telling me to call you. Couldn't figure out why he'd do that, unless the old ball-and-chain's somewhere connected with church."

Thanks a million, Bill. "Could I come over and see you?"

"Now? I'm pretty smelly from being out in the woods. Bagged me a five-point buck yesterday. Best hunting trip I've had in the last ten years. Anyway, I thought I'd take a shower and crawl into bed. Could we make it tomorrow?"

It occurred to me that Bill came by the toe-dragging act honestly. "This is something that can't wait."

"Not even till tomorrow? I took Monday off, too, so I won't be going to work. You could come by for coffee about nine."

"John, it really can't wait. Not even till then."

The silence lasted a full minute. "Nancy. It's about Nancy, isn't it?"

I took a deep breath and swallowed. "Yes."

"She left me, didn't she? Didn't even have the guts to tell me herself. Well, she can forget picking up her stuff. I'll just stuff it into garbage bags and leave it on the driveway for her to pick up when I'm not home. I'll get the locks changed tomorrow." He released a sound halfway between a laugh and a sob.

"John, Nancy's dead."

"Dead? She's healthy as a horse, and twice as likely to bite. You can't be serious."

Tears slid down my cheeks. He truly wasn't prepared for this. "I wish I didn't have to tell you this, but Nancy died this morning."

"Car accident? She gets a little dizzy from time to time, but her heart's fine. A stroke? Does Bill know? Of course he does. That's why he wanted me to call you. Probably too broke up to tell me himself."

"She died at church. Why don't I come over and tell you more about it?"

"Give me twenty minutes to shower and put on some clean clothes. Do you want me to get Bill over here, too?"

"No! No, I've already talked to Bill today." Bill's presence could only make this meeting more difficult for all of us.

"I can tell from your voice he's taking it pretty hard. Well, that's to be expected. See you in twenty minutes then."

As soon as I hung up, the phone jangled again, sending my nerves on a journey somewhere in the vicinity of the space station.

"You stood me up," Dora complained. "Do that to Ike Eichelberger and he'll haul your sorry rear down to Jessup and see you get some relaxation time as a guest of the state."

"Sorry. If this day doesn't end soon, I'm resigning from earth and moving to another planet."

"Yeah, planet hunk. I saw the way you caressed that poor, unsuspecting cop with your eyes." A series of crunches followed her cackle.

"I hear that. Are you eating potato chips?"

"Nofe. Harr sardough pressels."

"You shouldn't talk with your mouth full," I admonished.

A loud gulp punctuated our intellectual discussion. "That's the last one, too. I saved them for supper to share with a friend, but she never showed."

"Poor baby."

"And you dining in the finest style Thurmont has to offer. Where'd he take you? Wendy's or McDonald's? Cops aren't known for their fashionable taste in eating spots."

"He didn't come here to invite me to dinner, more's the pity. We went to the church so he could take another look and ask me some questions."

"Uh huh. A dark church, a cute young professional woman, a man with buns of steel . . . yeah, I'll bet he wanted to get you back to the scene of the crime."

"*Buns of steel*? Where'd that come from?"

Another snap of pretzel threatened to cloud her response. "Just because I'm old doesn't mean I'm blind, sweetie."

"Officer Eichelberger and I have a strictly professional relationship." Oh, Lord, have mercy on your sinful servant! My voice sounded so much like my mother's I almost turned around to make sure she hadn't walked in without knocking.

Not that it would ever occur to her to knock when entering her daughter's home. I knew my mother's motto: "Your house is my house."

"Well, you've got time to change that. Maybe you can think of some hot tidbits about Nancy Huff you can share with him. One per visit, of course."

Hot tidbits? About Nancy Huff? If anyone in the county knew them, Dora could ferret them out.

"Dora, have you heard any interesting gossip about Nancy lately?"

"Interesting gossip? That's one of those whatchacallits."

"An oxymoron?" I suggested.

"No, no. One of those things where you say the same thing twice."

"A redundancy."

"Yep. I haven't heard any *uninteresting* gossip since Eisenhower's presidency."

"Dora, I hate to gab and run, but I have to get over to John Huff's."

"He's too old for you. Besides, it's really bad form to chase a widower before they've lowered the wife's coffin into the ground. Especially when you're doing the burial."

I rolled my eyes so far up I thought I'd sprained my eyelids. "God has a special place in the next world for people who tease," I warned, "and it's not a nice, soft cloud."

"Well, at least I won't pine for lack of company. John wants to make the funeral arrangements already, huh?"

I found myself shaking my head, as if she could see that through the phone. "Dora, I'm not looking forward to this visit. He didn't know."

"Didn't know Nancy had died?" Her tone conveyed her disbelief. "You sure?"

"Positive, unless the man can act better than Harrison Ford. I had to break the news to him. Back to the gossip thing: do you know anything floating around about Nancy or John?"

"Let me check my sources and get back to you on that. Can't recall anything off the top of my head, but I haven't exactly followed Nancy as one of the most exciting residents of northern Frederick County. What kind of stories you looking for?"

I bit my lower lip. "I can't tell you that."

"Oh, goodie. That juicy, huh? This could be fun after all."

"Maybe we could get together for lunch tomorrow," I offered.

"Oh, no, you don't, sister! You had your chance. I'm not planning any more meals with you until I see the whites of your deviled eggs. By the way, you'd better put up some folding chairs for next Sunday."

"Folding chairs?"

"You bet. St. Luke's Church made the evening news on Baltimore TV. Fame has arrived."

I groaned. I'd hoped this would stay local. "Great."

"If you're headed over to the Huffs', you'd better get going instead of spending the whole evening yakking with some old lady."

With a laugh, a shake of my head, and a lightened heart, I picked up my purse and headed out the door.

If I hadn't known John was waiting for me, I might have thought his older brother had answered the door. He looked half a dozen years older than last Sunday.

"I called Bill, but he doesn't answer. You said he knows?"

"Yes. Everyone who came to St. Luke's for church this morning knows. Well, they may think they know more than they do, but they know Nancy died."

He sighed as if drawing his breath hurt. "Tell me how it happened."

"Someone killed her at the church."

He sat back in his chair as if he'd received a sudden blow. "Killed her? What do you mean?"

"I found her in the sacristy this morning. I assume she had planned to prepare for Communion, but someone apparently surprised her. From what I saw, I'd guess the person hit her from behind with the processional cross."

"One on one, Nancy could be sweeter than people ever guessed. But believe me, Nancy had one of the hardest heads this side of the Chesapeake Bay. That cross might have stunned her, but it wouldn't have killed her."

The image of Nancy lying under the paraments danced across my mind, taunting me with my powerlessness to undo this tragedy. "Some of the altar and pulpit cloths covered her face. Perhaps the killer smothered her to finish the job."

I walked over to his chair and placed my hand on his forearm. "John, I am so sorry. I can only tell you what I saw and my speculations about it. You can view the coroner's report in a day or two. In the meantime, we need to start making plans for Nancy's funeral."

I held his hand for the next several minutes as he cried silently, the tears rolling down his cheeks and neck, then disappearing beneath the collar of his shirt.

When the sorrow subsided, a look of intense hostility changed his face into a hard mask.

"She was stepping out on me, pastor. I know it. If they find the man she'd taken as her lover, they've got their killer."

Chapter Four

I didn't stay long with John Huff. He couldn't concentrate well enough to deal with funeral arrangements, and we couldn't have made any definite plans anyway without knowing when the coroner would release the body. Since he had a clear preference for a particular funeral home, I talked him through that call. The funeral director went out of his way to accommodate John and assure him he could handle the details no matter how long the authorities held onto the body.

Some things John did tell me. He wanted no part of cremation for his wife. Though I thought the damage to her head might make a viewing less desirable, I wouldn't have contradicted his wishes. However, when he asked my advice on the best place to purchase a headstone, I pleaded complete ignorance. He took me back to their bedroom and showed me her closet, begging me to help him pick appropriate attire for the coffin. Remembering what Suzie had said, I suggested a tan suit with a cream blouse.

I took notes on favorite hymns, best-loved scriptures, and even menu items for the funeral luncheon. Nancy had hated ham salad, so we would avoid serving that. She also loathed dill pickles, but John adored them, so we agreed to let them appear on the fellowship hall tables after the burial.

Then I made a call to the man in charge of the church's cemetery. He agreed to call John back in the morning with information about opening the grave, installing the head-stone, and providing for what the cemetery committee insisted on calling "perpetual care." He even had a hint on which tombstone company to avoid because they often confused digits in the dates, resulting in the deceased sometimes appearing to have died before coming into the world.

When I finally arrived home, I threw my purse in the direction of the couch. I ignored the protesting smack it made when it hit the wall and dropped items of clothing along the way to my bed. My mother's voice reminded me how awful that would look if I died during the night and someone else had to pick up after me. I ignored that, too. I figured it would spare them making a decision what to put on me in my coffin. I fell asleep to the strains of Mozart's "Dies Irae" on my CD player. I felt sure Nancy wouldn't have chosen that piece for her funeral, and I doubted John had ever heard of it. I hoped it wouldn't become the theme song for my week.

Amazingly, I woke refreshed and bursting with energy. I boiled a dozen eggs as I made and ate breakfast, determined Dora wouldn't catch me unprepared if she called by lunchtime with some information from the Frederick County grapevine. If she wanted to see the whites of my deviled eggs, I'd have them sitting on an appropriately shaped plate, ready to stare right back at her.

The phone rang. A polite voice from the state police barracks informed me we could clean up the sacristy, so I phoned the altar guild vice president and asked her to let the other members know.

I generally take Mondays off, but I had the feeling I'd better get ahead in my work, since I supposed I'd have a funeral later in the week. Probably about the time I usually wrote my Sunday sermon.

I tore into the task at full speed, scratching notes on a yellow legal pad as I read two versions of the scripture, checked my favorite commentary on the gospel lesson, and pretended I remembered enough Greek to examine possible textual difficulties in the original. Then I pounded out a rough draft on my computer. I had just saved it when the phone jangled again.

"Pastor Abby, this is Charlotte Baker. Do you think you could help Celia Martin and me clean up the mess those state police made? There's black dust all over the sacristy. We'll look like coalminers before we have this place straightened up. I know you take Mondays off, but I can't find anyone else from the altar guild at home."

I looked longingly in the direction of the kitchen, where my dozen eggs awaited their transformation. There went my chance for a lunch at Dora's, complete with an update on her information seeking. When it came to local gossip, I'd put Dora Knaub up against any search engine in the computer universe for speed and efficiency.

Then I remembered Charlotte was one of Nancy's closest friends. While Celia and Nancy hadn't seemed particularly chummy, the late altar guild president had once worked as a paralegal for Celia's husband Tom before he retired from the bench. At worst, maybe they could come up with some anecdotes I could include in Nancy's funeral homily.

Charlotte hadn't lied about the grime. She and Celia looked like two kindergartners who'd just destroyed a box of licorice sticks. A bucket filled with wet, sooty-looking rags stood on the spot where I'd found Nancy's body.

"I suppose they had to do this to find fingerprints," Charlotte complained as soon as she saw me in the doorway, "but I can't see what good it will do. They'll only find prints from the altar guild members, and they certainly couldn't suspect any of us."

I hummed one of my vague sounds meant to suggest agreement without committing me to it. Celia Martin gave me a knowing look.

"What can I help with?" I asked.

"You could empty this bucket and get us some fresh water?" Charlotte said. "No sense you getting as grimed up as we must look."

"I'll do that," a deep voice offered. I turned to face Tom Martin, looking every bit the retired judge, even in a ratty sweater and jeans worn at the knees. His distinguished air still commanded respect in our congregation and across the county.

"Thanks, Tom." I put on the gloves I kept in my office for handling the church's brass and silver articles.

Charlotte puffed up like a small blowfish. "Well, I declare, how downright inconsiderate of those cops to mess up the place we keep our church's most revered belongings. What is this world coming to, when even the police act so rude?"

"Just doing their job," Tom suggested.

"Of course you'd say that," Charlotte snapped. "You spent all those years in law enforcement yourself. And you don't have to put the things they've messed up back in order."

Tom's hearty laugh echoed off the walls. "I know a lot of police officers who'd take exception to your insistence that I belong in the same category they do. My decisions didn't always meet with their approval."

It struck me that I knew very little about Tom or his term on the bench. He'd already retired when I arrived at St. Luke's. I made a mental note to ask Dora what she knew about him and why Nancy had stopped working for him.

Tom toted away the bucket, brought fresh water, and took the used rags to his car to wash them at home. We soon had the place shining.

Celia offered to help me replace the heavy pulpit bible on the bottom shelf of the heritage cabinet. When we lifted it, she stumbled against the glass door, shaking it so it rattled like a California crystal shop in an earthquake.

Tom grabbed her and pulled her against his solid chest. "Are you all right, honey? Did you hurt yourself?"

The fine lines around her mouth tightened. In a slightly exasperated tone, she replied, "I have MS, Tom. I'm not a paraplegic."

He stroked her face with the fingertips of his left hand. "Oh, I know you're tough as nails. But I've made it my job to protect you."

While they looked into one another's eyes for a moment, I wondered if I would ever experience that level of relationship. I tried to imagine E. Eichelberger running his fingers gently down my cheeks, but instead I got a picture of him holding out a pair of handcuffs.

"If you lovebirds have finished grossing out our pastor, you can get out of here," Charlotte said with a snicker. "I'll get her to help me put back the last of the paraments. Then we've got things all ready to go till Christmas Eve."

I asked the Martins if they could remember any stories about Nancy I could use in the funeral homily, and Tom told me some events that had happened at the courthouse.

After thanking the Martins for their help and waving to them from my office window as they climbed into their SUV, I ran back to the sacristy and grabbed my end of the white and gold frontal that would decorate our altar for the coming sacred celebration.

Just when I felt ready to get down to some serious talk with Charlotte about Nancy, the cordless phone I'd brought from the office vibrated, rattling furiously on the glass-covered counter. We stared at it as if it were a cobra that had crept in while our backs were turned.

"Better get the damn thing," Charlotte grumbled.

I did. "St. Luke's, Pastor Abby speaking."

"You got anything in that wasteland you call a kitchen besides saltines and canned soup?" Dora demanded.

"Give me twenty minutes and I'll have a surprise for you."

"In your case, anything edible would qualify as a surprise." She cackled at her own joke. "Hurry it up. I made a few calls and hit pay dirt. I'll bring some scrapple."

I shuddered. If the person who put the food together couldn't tell for sure what was in it, I wanted no part of it. "Keep that for yourself. What do you say to grilled cheese sandwiches?"

"I say what I have for you deserves better than the burnt offering you'll plunk down in front of me, but I'm a forgiving and long-suffering woman, so you're in luck. I have some leftover slippery pot pie, but won't you at least try the scrapple? It's from Dorsey's butcher shop."

Even if it came from Queen Elizabeth's kitchen at Windsor Castle, I had no intention of touching the stuff. "I'll decline that delight," I said.

"You don't know what you're missing. You're going to be so grateful when you hear what I've got you'll offer to eat hog maw every night for a week, with fried brains for dessert."

I moaned. "I doubt the universe holds that much gratitude. See you later."

I turned to Charlotte, who was losing a wrestling match with her coat. Why hadn't I noticed before how much weight she'd gained in the last year? Either the increase had occurred gradually, or I'd floated away from reality more than I'd thought.

"Charlotte, I know you and Nancy were close. Could you spare me some time today or tomorrow to tell me about her? I need some stories I can share at the funeral."

Charlotte colored. "I suppose so. Probably better to get it over with. I heard you on the phone, so I know you've got a luncheon date. That cop who investigated the murder?"

If only my Internet provider had the reliability and the speed of the northern Frederick County gossip grapevine!

"No, my neighbor."

"Oh, sure. Dora Knaub, right? Nice old lady, even if she does have a mouth on her like one of those television wrestlers."

Somehow I had difficulty picturing Charlotte sitting down front of her TV, beer in hand, to watch WWF on pay-per-view.

"Would you prefer to talk to me on the phone, come back here, or have me drop by your house early this afternoon?" I asked.

"Come to my place. I have some housework to catch up on, so that would work a lot better for me."

For some reason, Charlotte wanted the safety of her home turf. No problem. I only needed a few more stories about the late Mrs. Huff.

After I heard the rumble of Charlotte's ancient green Buick gasping its way out of the parking lot, I inspected the heritage cabinet one last time. We'd done good work, but the communion vessels from the other church didn't look right. I tried shifting them around. No improvement. Then I noticed the ciborium looked tilted. Could something have unbalanced it? I lifted the cross-topped lid. Nothing in there. What had I expected, century-old communion wafers?

Its stem leaned to one side, so I picked it up and tapped its bottom sharply against the shelf. Now it matched the chalice—both a little bent in spots, but all the more precious for the years of use reflected in each nick and scratch.

Chopping like a demented sushi chef, I turned out a fine-looking plate of deviled eggs in fifteen minutes flat. Face it: for me, gourmet cooking meant a few torn pieces of fresh parsley floating on my canned chicken noodle soup. I quickly sprinkled the eggs with a little paprika, plunked the skillet on the stovetop, and threw the cheese and bread on the cutting board.

Dora came in carrying a picnic basket and smiling suspiciously. What culinary horrors lay under that wicker cover? I shuddered in anticipation.

Speechless, Dora gaped at the egg plate on the table. "Who are these supposed to be, your church board?"

"Now, do any of them have horns and evil grins?" I asked.

"Actually, you may have a different answer to that after I share some of the dirt I dug up."

My stomach lurched and threatened to dislodge the lunch I hadn't yet eaten.

Sensing my uneasiness, Dora hurried to reassure me. "Hey, you know how I go on. Nothing's *that* bad. First things first. Let's eat. I think I'll start with this horny little devil."

She picked up one of my creations with wispy celery whiskers, red pepper mouth and horns, and olive chunks marking the eyes and nose. "I reckoned the scrapple was a lost cause, but I still have hope I can win you over on slippery pot pie." She pulled a casserole out of her basket and lifted the lid. A rich, meaty smell wafted through the room.

Then I looked into the dish. "What have you got here, something snails have been swimming in?" I said.

Dora propped her fists on her hips. "I should grab a knife and scrape your tongue, since you obviously have impaired taste buds. Not that this kitchen would have anything sharp enough." She shook her head in mock disgust.

"We'll share the eggs." I tried to placate her; after all, I was eager to hear what she'd learned. "Haven't we had enough culinary chitchat to proceed to the news of the day?" I begged.

"I suppose. Turns out one of my sources had the goods on Nancy Huff. Sort of," Dora hedged.

"Stop torturing me and spill the beans!" I urged.

"This certain someone—a very reliable source, and discreet enough that her story hasn't made the usual rounds—

saw Nancy in a hole-in-the-wall kind of place up near Gettysburg. With a man."

I bit another deviled egg in half. "A man other than John Huff."

"You got it. At least four times."

Dora extracted a freshly baked apple pie from her basket. She didn't really have to worry about getting into heaven. Not because of her good heart, though that couldn't hurt. When she died, Dora could just show up at the pearly gates with one of her apple pies. She could bribe her way into heaven, because no one this side of God could resist that dessert.

When her hands shook as she covered the pie and stuck it in my refrigerator, I knew she had more to tell me, something more disturbing.

"You've distracted me long enough with the evidence of your baking skills. Name the man seen with Nancy, and we'll forgive him his bad taste."

"Yeah, that place my friend saw them in doesn't make meals much better than you do."

I stared her down. "Why are you having such a hard time telling me the name of this guy?"

She shrugged and glanced quickly out the window. "Frank Teller."

"That name doesn't mean a thing to me. I don't know him."

Dora took my hand. "You know his daughter. Suzie."

"Suzie Huff?" I shouted. "Bill's wife? John and Nancy's daughter-in-law?" That certainly put the toe dragging and plate processions of the previous day in a new light.

"Yep. Doesn't look so good for old John, does it?"

"Maybe not. If Teller killed Nancy, the police may clear John right away."

"We can hope. Unfortunately, it also gives John a logical reason for wanting his wife dead."

She took a deep breath and continued. "I wish I didn't have any other bad news for you."

Disaster loomed like a rhinoceros standing on the front porch, ringing the doorbell.

"Go on." I couldn't get anything more out.

"Another one of my calls uncovered some sleazy actions by your board president."

"Sleazy? Alvin Porter?"

"Abby, he wants to get rid of you and has plans to win your bishop over to his side. He's telling people you're incompetent and not fit to hold the office of pastor."

I slapped my palms on my temples and dropped my elbows against the table edge. Winter has its advantages, because in the spring the neighbors would have heard my moans through the open windows and called 911. I shook my head in agony. How could I combat Alvin with everything else I had to get done in the next few weeks?

Then I realized I had just dragged my hair through the remains of ice cream, apple pie, and deviled egg on my plate.

Chapter Five

After a quick shower to remove any food remnants from my hair, I headed for the Bakers' house. In spite of the icy wind, I didn't bother to turn on the car's heater. As long as I thought about Alvin and his plans for me, the steam pouring from my ears would keep the car toasty warm.

The low, swiftly moving clouds created a rolling pattern of shadows on Catoctin Mountain's slope, making the leafless forest appear to undulate like waves on the Atlantic shore. Thinking of the hot water I could land in if the bishop caught wind of Alvin's accusations, I felt my body temperature drop and turned the heater on after all.

The breeze picked up as I turned onto the road where the Bakers lived. Tree branches waved to me as I passed, and the last of autumn's leaves kissed my windshield on their way to the thicket on my right.

My worry about recognizing Charlotte's house disappeared as I made the first curve. Charlotte had made good use of the weekend: the Seven Dwarfs, decked out in red and green striped sweaters over their ceramic bodies, rang bells and shook holly branches on one side of her drive. On the other, Donald Duck, his three nephews, and Uncle Scrooge held out elaborately wrapped presents to welcome visitors. How had Charlotte moved the figures? They had to weigh a ton.

Her hair still wet from the shower and proudly sporting

a green and red sweatsuit with scattered patterns of gold stars, silver bells, and snowmen, Charlotte met me at the door to her breezeway looking much more relaxed than she had at the church.

"Come in, Pastor," she greeted me. "I have some nice hickory bark and kumquat tea brewing."

Oh, goody, my favorite. "Thanks for the offer, but I just ate an enormous lunch."

"Don't be silly. This will help everything settle just right."

Or bring it up on the family room rug. I glanced down. Hundreds of little crocheted Rudolph faces stared up at me. "You've already finished your Christmas decorating?"

"Well, the last pastor told us every year we should observe Advent and save the Christmas decorating until the last moment. But I can't. As soon as the supermarkets start selling Thanksgiving turkeys, I have to get my Christmas stuff out and set it up. I have so much of it I could never put it all together in a day or two. Take this rug, for example."

Take it? Not on your life. "Unique. I've never seen one like it."

"You never will, either. Took me a couple of hours every winter night four years ago to crochet the Rudolphs." She sighed. "I had plans for this rug, to use it as a demonstration piece in my craft shop. But that Nancy story wouldn't interest you. You want something appropriate for her funeral, right?"

"Yes, maybe something sort of personal."

Charlotte plopped onto a couch covered completely by embroidered pillows featuring sleeping kittens and puppies entwined in Christmas wrappings. She motioned me toward a Boston rocker decorated with cushions sporting bunnies dressed like Santa. I'd never had the feeling of Christmas closing in on me in such a physical sense.

"Let's see what I can find that you might use." Charlotte

leafed through a diary with a cross-stitched bouquet on the front.

"No, not this one. She treated that poor woman like a shark would a tuna sandwich. How about the time she made cork reindeer for all the parish children and gave them out at the Sunday School Christmas party?"

She put a bookmark in the book and handed it to me before trotting into her kitchen. I should have expected the bookmark: a crocheted string with a ceramic reindeer hoof attached.

"It has gotten a little chilly in here, hasn't it?" Charlotte said as she plunked down the Currier and Ives tray holding the cups and teapot. Of course the knitted tea cozy resembled a poinsettia, if a somewhat droopy one.

A quick glance told me the story wasn't what I needed, so I closed the diary and set it on the coffee table.

I accepted the offered teacup and sipped. Not bad, if you liked fruity bark water.

Obviously I needed to switch approaches or resign myself to muttering platitudes about Nancy's commitment to her church and family. "Tell me about the Nancy the rest of us never got to know."

Charlotte choked on her hickory bark and kumquat tea. Just when I thought I'd need to slap her on the back a few dozen times, she recovered enough to put her tea down on the coffee table, the saucer brimming with liquid the color of moldy rust. "Since we had such a long friendship, I should have a whole boatload of stories about wonderful and generous things my great pal did, right?"

At last I seemed headed toward my strongest need for the rest of this week, an anchor story for my funeral homily. "Well maybe not a boatload. One or two stories that show Nancy's finer qualities—"

The howl from Charlotte startled and disturbed me. Grief at the loss of her friend I had expected, but this struck me as extreme. Then I looked a little closer at the tears coursing down her cheeks. Sobs of laughter, not sorrow, poured from the shaking woman in front of me.

"Finer qualities. You bet. Let me tell you my favorite Nancy Huff story of all time." The sarcasm dripped from her voice like acid from a leaky battery.

Charlotte stood and began to pace back and forth across the length of the room. "No doubt you've noticed I'm something of an expert at crafts."

I nodded vigorously, hoping my acknowledgement of the crafts would save me from having to endorse her expertise.

"About a year ago, I told Nancy my plans to open my own country crafts store. I had in mind a nice, airy space full of things my friends and I would make. Since Nancy made things of comparable quality to mine, I thought she'd be a natural partner in the business. Besides handmade items, we'd carry scrapbooking supplies."

She waved at the cluttered collection of artifacts sitting on every flat space. Comparing her homey but rough crafts with Nancy's works of art struck me as similar to declaring Wal-Mart on the same level as Neiman Marcus, but I grunted one of my all-purpose syllables and hoped she wouldn't press the issue. I couldn't imagine Nancy considering Charlotte her equal at craftwork.

"And she had inherited some money from her aunt earlier that year, so the two of us together could come up with the money to start the shop. I found an ideal spot, cheap for its location because the previous renter had gone out of business. Nancy got the money out of the bank. She even showed me the cashier's check."

The tears slipping past each side of Charlotte's mouth no longer had any connection with laughter. I reached into my purse and handed her a tissue. "Something happened. You never opened the store," I guessed.

She blew her nose with a sound that reminded me of the whistle of the train going through my grandmother's village in the middle of summer nights.

"She showed the plans to that fancy-shmancy lawyer she works for. Worked for. According to her, Briggs talked her out of it. Meanwhile, I went ahead and signed the lease. Then I found out she had dumped the whole project. When I asked her to help pay for the lease, she laughed. She said Briggs told her she had no legal liability because we hadn't signed any contract or partnership instrument."

Another honk. I offered her a fresh tissue, but she shook her head. She crammed the used one into a jar holding an unlit candle. "Partnership instrument. I'll never forget her expression when she said that. How I wished for a real instrument, something nice and sharp. I swear I would have cut that smirk right off her face."

I began to picture pieces of Nancy's crewel and cross-stitch and some of the beautiful bouquets she had arranged. This homily would definitely center on accomplishments and energy rather than personal qualities.

Charlotte picked up a painted cardboard angel with tinsel hair and an aluminum foil halo. She crushed it, dropped it on the rug, and ground it with her foot.

"I dreamed about having a shop of my own for years. I'd planned and waited. She ruined it. She ruined me. I hated the witch," she whispered. "I can't make myself, even for a minute, feel sorry she's dead."

Had Charlotte murdered her former friend? In her mind, she had reason enough. Nancy wouldn't have blinked an eye at her presence in the church, since they both served on the altar guild.

On the other hand, the room had provided the means of Nancy's death. At least that appeared true, and I hadn't heard anything to contradict that assumption.

I hadn't heard from Officer Eichelberger. Probably wouldn't. The conversation with Charlotte was privileged anyway, so I didn't have a pretense for calling him myself.

Back home, I flung myself into the ratty armchair I had

rescued from a yard sale. It matched perfectly with my naturally distressed desk with the drawers that didn't fit no matter how I rotated them. Together with the steel bookshelves meant for garage storage, my lovely desk and chair had helped me achieve the ideal decorating effect for my life: early attic.

After two hours of penance preparing my confirmation class lessons for the rest of the month, I sat down with my personal calendar to plot my pre-Christmas visitations to shut-ins and nursing homes. That didn't go well. I couldn't write in specific dates yet, since I had to save time for Nancy's funeral but couldn't schedule that until the coroner released her body and the funeral home made its arrangements.

The phone rang. As if by some grand design or mental telepathy, the funeral director informed me they planned to pick up Nancy's body Wednesday afternoon. Could I do the funeral at St. Luke's on Friday? The funeral home would hold visiting hours the night before. So John had decided on a church funeral after all. Apparently my powers of persuasion worked better than I thought.

I spent the next hour tracking down our church organist to see if he could play for Nancy's funeral. Warren Weston's musical talent exceeded the whining he does when he has to change his schedule, but not by much. After a dozen threats not to show and an equal number of pleas from me, he finally agreed. Probably just to get off the phone.

I understood Warren's reluctance. He owned his own investment brokerage, and his work piled up toward the end of the week.

The matter of his conflicts with Nancy didn't help. Warren's choices for organ and choral music seemed a little esoteric to the people in St. Luke's pews, who wanted to hear the same things they'd heard as children. Nancy caught him on his way out the door more than one Sunday morning and took him to task over the hymns or a piece of music. He learned to respond two ways. Sometimes he blamed me—a technique I greatly appreciated—and sometimes he informed her that a person of her low tastes simply couldn't appreciate sublime music.

Thinking back over their running battle, I concluded Nancy might stand accused if someone had murdered Warren, but not the other way around. Then again, Warren really, really didn't take criticism well.

For the next three days, I ran around northern Frederick County in a whirlwind of visitations. Not one of the shut-ins living at home refrained from asking for the gory details of Nancy Huff's demise. Most of them considered Phyllis Huff, John's mother and a frequent target of Nancy's complaints, an old friend, so the sympathy expressed fell mostly into the "such a young person to pass" or "such a horrible way to go" category.

Thursday we got our first covering of snow, just the right amount to make the back roads slippery. Though I hoped my road wouldn't freeze over before I returned from the funeral home, I marveled again at the silence snow brought, even in an already quiet rural area. The bushes looked like giant snowballs, and I wished Charlotte would take them as inspiration for some of her crafts instead of resorting to tacky knockoffs of Disney characters and folk-art attempts constructed from materials found in the kitchen or garbage can.

No wonder Nancy had changed her mind about a business association with her old friend, though she had severed the ties in rather harsh fashion, if Charlotte's tale had any resemblance to the truth.

To my surprise, the parking lot at the funeral home and both adjoining streets overflowed with cars when I arrived some twenty minutes early. I found a spot and slid rather than walked down the street to my destination.

As often happens at these events, clusters of relatives and

friends had formed in the corner. I made my way through the receiving line, hugged John and Bill and Suzie as I expressed my condolences, and checked on a few last-minute details. We had played answering machine tag the last few days and had settled the fine points for the service that way.

Dora Knaub sidled up to me and pulled my elbow so she could more easily whisper in my ear. "Don't look now, but the man standing with Barb Johnson is Frank Teller."

Of course, I immediately scanned the room to find Barb.

Dora pinched me. "I told you not to look!"

"Then how will I know who you mean?" I responded.

"At least have the subtlety to stand facing me and pretend we're talking while you stare at him."

"We are having a conversation," I insisted.

"If this is a conversation, I'm Oprah Winfrey."

"Good. Could you lend me a million or two from your petty cash? I'd love to build my own house and get out of the parsonage. Shucks, I'd love to furnish the parsonage with something other than flea market rejects."

She shook her head in mock disgust. "What's the church coming to? A pastor conducting herself this way during a member's viewing."

"I'll try to do better when she's on show before the service at St. Luke's tomorrow." I crossed my heart and rolled my eyes heavenward.

"You're incorrigible."

"I know. Ask my mother if you question it."

"What do you think?"

"Of Frank Teller? He looks like Tom Brokaw after he's spent a couple of months camping in the Rockies."

"Bingo. He's a crew boss for one of the biggest construction companies in the county."

Another glance around the room revealed people I knew reasonably well after just a year and a half in the area. Except for one. I murmured goodbye to Dora and squeezed through the crowd to where Celia and Tom Martin stood with a man I didn't know.

"Hello," I greeted them. "The flowers look lovely. Nancy would have appreciated them."

Celia and Tom nodded, but the stranger laughed quietly. "More likely she would have rearranged them all. Take the one with all the orchids. She would spread those out among the various bunches."

I held out my hand. "I'm Abigail Shaw, Nancy's pastor." A superfluous detail, with my clerical collar in plain view.

"George Briggs," he answered. He shook my hand so vigorously I thought he might dislocate my wrist. "Nancy worked as a paralegal in my office."

Aha. The boss. Too late now to pick his brain for a good homily story that put Nancy in a favorable light. Or maybe not.

My hope for a better sermon illustration went down the drain when John Huff motioned me to join him in the small hallway near the restrooms.

"Pastor Abby, I need to talk to you first thing tomorrow morning."

"Of course. But you look terribly worried. What's wrong?"

He grimaced and checked over his shoulder to make sure no one overheard us. "I found out this afternoon the police have a witness who can place me in town the morning Nancy died."

Chapter Six

In spite of my best efforts, I didn't manage to keep my jaw from dropping open.

"Tell me that again." With luck, I had misheard him.

"Someone saw me here Sunday morning."

I grabbed John's tie and dragged him over to the women's room, intending to pull him into it so we could have some privacy. Barb Johnson flung open the door at that moment, saw us standing there, and looked at me as if I had just handed her a bag full of fresh roadkill.

"Nice tie," I ad-libbed, patting the rack of gold deer antlers against a solid red background.

"Nancy gave it to me last Christmas. It seemed appropriate," he answered.

Barb's eyes widened in her patented "you've lost your mind" expression. She shook her head twice, the way you do to discourage gnats, and took off at full speed for the viewing parlor. She glanced back once, apparently to make sure she hadn't imagined us.

I pulled open the only unmarked door in the small hallway. From the couch and stuffed chairs, and the presence of full boxes of tissues on every non-upholstered flat surface, I knew this had to be the private grief room. I motioned John inside, shut the door, and turned the lock.

"A case of mistaken identity, right?" Every fiber of my brain sent out the message that he should agree with me.

"Uh, well . . . no."

So much for my skill at transmitting mental messages. There went my future as a psychic if Alvin Porter succeeded in his crusade to have the bishop dismiss me.

"Someone did see you in Thurmont."

"Yep."

"Sunday morning."

"Yep."

Overwhelmed by a sinking feeling, I checked the floor. It didn't seem any farther from the ceiling than before.

"I thought you went deer hunting in Pennsylvania."

He shrugged. "I did. But the more I sat up there in the woods, the more Nancy's carrying on with some guy back here bothered me. I decided I had to find out who he was and what they were doing behind my back. So I snuck into town before sunrise and tried to follow her. I hid in the woods across from our house and used my field glasses. But I never saw her leave home."

He jumped up from his chair and walked over to the window, though I guessed he couldn't see anything outside in the dark, not even the streetlight directly in front of the funeral home. "I checked the garage. No car. I almost went crazy imagining she had spent the weekend with him, whoever he is—was. I drove past some of our relatives' and some of her friends' homes."

A shiver of fear crept up my spine.

"Then you went to the church."

With the speed of a frightened doe, he spun around to face me and laughed. "No. It never occurred to me she'd gone there. Maybe I fell asleep watching the house and she left without me seeing her. I went back to the mountains, figuring I could at least get a day of hunting in."

He grabbed his tie and gave it a swing. "I always did have better luck in the woods than I had with Nancy." His smile disappeared. "You believe me, Pastor, don't you?"

"Yes." For some reason, I did believe him, but I had my

doubts the authorities would share my conviction. If I had found out the name of Nancy's other interest, the police would, too. If they hadn't already. John needed a good lawyer.

My pastoral need to take care of him at this difficult juncture in his life overrode my desire to give him advice. Perhaps the police needed a lot more than one report of his presence in town to proceed against him. Getting him and the rest of Nancy's family and friends through the burial service in the morning had to be my first priority.

When we entered the viewing room, I felt as if everyone in the place stared at us, wondering why we'd left the viewing for so long. I patted John on the shoulder and whispered, "I think this would be an excellent time for a public prayer."

A quizzical expression crossed his face until the light dawned and he gave me a curt nod. Using my best ministerial voice, I invited the assembled viewers to join us in prayer for the Huff family in the midst of their tragedy. *In the midst of life we are in death.* Where had I ever heard that? An old service book, most likely. I had the creepiest feeling it would apply to me for the foreseeable future.

On my way through the foyer, a hand seized my shoulder. "We need to talk," a voice whispered.

I looked up into the deep blue eyes, underscored with a bridge of freckles, of my favorite state trooper.

"Trooper Eichelberger?" I asked, not because I didn't recognize him, but because of my surprise at his presence in this context.

"Yeah. Guess I look different out of uniform."

He looked even more luscious than he had on Sunday. What did that man lift to make those biceps stand out that way? Squad cars? Hippopotamuses?

"You're looking gor—looking well," I said. First a string of sour events marched into my life just as we supposedly ushered in the happiest time of the year. (Ha! Pastors knew better.) Now my tongue had decided to bypass my brain.

"Do you often attend funerals where you plan to arrest one of the bereaved shortly?" I asked.

His wide eyes told me I'd hit home.

"I can't give you any information about that sort of thing. We do often go to the viewing or funeral of a murdered person. You'd be surprised what hints we pick up that way."

"Walk me to my car," I ordered.

We slid along the icy sidewalk. When I slipped and imitated a windmill in an attempt to prevent a humiliating sprawl on the ground, he encased my shoulders with his arm and pulled me against him.

And the theologians at the seminary talked about Holy Communion as a foretaste of heaven!

Where could my mind have gone? I had a parishioner probably headed for jail, a board president who wanted my head on a pike at the entrance to the church parking lot, and a lousy funeral homily.

"Do you really have enough evidence to try John Huff for murder?" I asked. I felt rather than saw him shrug.

"The legal eagles decide that. But I can say things look pretty bad for him. Look, you can't share this with anyone. Two people positively identified him as present right here in town on Sunday morning. He hid that fact from us. In fact, he still hasn't admitted being here."

We stopped walking and faced one another. His arm dropped to his side, and my shoulders ached at the desertion. "The witnesses could be mistaken."

He shoved his hands in his pockets, which made his biceps strain against the sleeves of his suit. "Not likely. One of them works with John. The other guy's known him for thirty years."

"That's enough to arrest him?" I didn't really expect him

to tell me what else they might have against John Huff, but what harm could asking do?

"He had the opportunity. He had access to the church, and it makes sense both that he would have gone there to talk to his wife and that they had words. He had a motive, too."

"No one would describe her as easy to live with," I admitted.

"He had better reasons than that. I can't tell you more."

That could mean he knew about the threat to kill her that Bill had told me about, or it could imply they'd found out about Frank Teller. Or both. Or other things I had no inkling of.

When I unlocked my car, Officer Eichelberger assisted me from the icy curb into the driver's seat with one hand at the small of my back and the other under my forearm. A jolt shot through me, and I couldn't decide whether static or chemistry had supplied the electricity.

Friday morning dawned gray and windy. The temperature had climbed enough to turn the occasional snow flurries into icy rain. The men from the funeral home had difficulty negotiating the coffin into the church, and it slipped off its bier and crashed to the floor as soon as they got inside.

Luckily no one else had arrived, leaving me as the only witness. The funeral director apologized profusely, and I assured him we'd concentrate on just getting through the morning. His assistants hurried the casket to the front of the church and opened the lid.

When they saw the mess the fall had made of Nancy's hair, they pressed me into emergency beauty repair duty. I located my purse, pulled out a comb, and made a valiant attempt to make her look less squashed. I bit back a giggle at the thought of the fury she would have exhibited at such a personal affront.

The funeral director gave me a pitying look. "I suppose that's the best you can manage." If Nancy had seen the results of my feeble efforts, she would have come back with a much stronger remark.

I gave him the smile I display as the children come up for the children's sermon—welcoming but no nonsense. "I got my degree in theology, not cosmetology."

He blew out a long breath. "You conduct a beautiful burial service, and you definitely made the right career decision." His eyes went back to the head in the coffin, and I caught him check a shake of his head.

All services have their own atmosphere, and the context of this one guaranteed a high degree of tension. The relatives on Nancy's side of the family stewed and steamed near the back of the church on the left side. I noticed Suzie sat between John and Bill in the front right pew and that the two men exchanged only a few words during the entire proceedings.

Since St. Luke's cemetery, which stretched behind and to one side of the church's lawn, contained the Huff burial plot, we slipped and slid across the ice-coated grass and gravel roadways to the tent erected shortly after dawn by the mortuary employees.

Aware of the stiff breeze, I quickly moved the service through its graveside portion and herded the few brave souls who had left the shelter of the church inside to the fellowship hall for the funeral luncheon. Nancy's sister and mother sat where they could glare at John, but they pointedly managed not to speak a word to him when they came over to his table to greet Bill and Suzie. I looked around for Frank Teller but couldn't find him. Perhaps he had come to the service and had already left.

I wandered from table to table, speaking to my parishioners and asking them to introduce me to the mourners I didn't know. Several had worked with Nancy. Relatives made up the rest, underscoring the absence of personal friends.

When I noticed John and Bill exchanging quiet but obviously snappy words with one another, I floated over to their spot. "How are you doing, John?" I asked.

"I've had better days." He gave Bill a look clearly meant as a reprimand. Bill opened his mouth to respond but clamped it shut when Suzie seized his forearm and squeezed.

John shoved back his chair. The squeak of the rubber feet of the chair legs on the tile floor almost covered his deep sigh. "Apparently I've already been tried and convicted as a criminal. Even by people in my family."

Bill got up and walked toward the parking lot exit. Suzie mumbled an apology, gathered up their coats, and took off after him.

"I take it you mean your son," I said.

"He hasn't said it directly, but he's dropped little hints all morning."

If I could have gotten my hands on Bill's lapels at that point, I would have shaken him like a dusty throw rug. I understood his grief, but his father needed support to get through this day. Of course, I knew something Bill didn't, that the police might arrest John at any time. Unless things had changed and they'd found another suspect or had decided the evidence didn't justify such action, but I didn't kid myself about the likelihood of that.

"Pastor, I feel as if you're the only one in my corner."

"You can take that to the bank, John. Your family will support you too." As soon as the words left my lips, I knew what cold comfort they'd provide. The only family backing he needed or wanted had just walked out of the church. The sense of desertion showed in his eyes and in the tightness around his mouth.

Celia Martin came over to the table and hugged John. "If we can do anything to help, give us a call. We know how terrible this is for you." As she left, she stood out of John's line of sight and motioned to me to follow.

After excusing myself, I stopped at the next table to talk to Nancy's boss, George Briggs. Then I crossed to the rear of the hall and sat down across from Celia and Tom.

"Well, tell her," Celia prompted.

Tom grimaced. "You're not going to like this."

I held my palms up in a gesture of surrender to the fates. "A lot of things happen I don't like, but I can't control them, so I just accept them and go on."

Tom nodded his approval of my response. "Please don't share this with anyone, but the state police will arrest John Huff this afternoon for Nancy's murder."

With his connections at the courthouse, Tom's access to this information didn't surprise me. "Do you think I should ask George Briggs to suggest a colleague who'd do a good job of defending John?"

Tom pulled his lower lip in between his teeth and glanced down at his shoes. "Don't think I'd do that, Pastor Abby. Unlike me when she worked in my office, George never minded Nancy's—ah, prickliness, and he appreciated the way she did her work for him. Efficiency was her biggest strength."

"You think he'll take sides against John," I suggested.

"I meant he won't want to get involved, but you may have the right idea there. A lot of people will turn against John as soon as they clamp the cuffs on him." He pantomimed the action.

"Tom!" Celia warned. "Lots of people will rush to his defense, too. The way Nancy treated him, out in the open and in his face, won him a great deal of sympathy here at St. Luke's. And you know yourself how hard she was to work with. It'll surprise me if both his coworkers and hers don't start a defense fund."

By the time I finally arrived home after the funeral, I felt as if twelve Clydesdales had dragged my weary body behind them for twelve hours, over cobbled streets, down gravel lanes, and through their leavings. I tore off my clothes, threw them in the general direction of the hamper, and fell rather than stepped into the shower. I leaned against the wall and let the water pound against me until I had depleted the supply of hot water and the cold water woke me up enough to crawl out and collapse on my bed.

Then the phone rang. I had just decided to ignore it and let the machine pick up when I remembered the state police planned to arrest John that afternoon. Could they have moved in so quickly after the funeral?

"St. Luke's parsonage, Pastor Abby speaking." I pushed the words through my exhaustion into the phone.

"You sound more like the one who got buried than the person who did the burying," Dora Knaub said. "I figured this would happen. You've flown around this week like a blind bird looking for a worm."

"I've had about that much success," I admitted.

I pushed the hair off my forehead and pulled my hand across my scalp to the base of my neck.

"What would you say to a nice bowl or two of chicken corn soup?" Dora asked.

"Throw in a salad and I'll worship at your feet."

"Better not, Pastor. Alvin Porter would love to add the worship of false gods to his charges against you." She cackled.

Alvin. I knew something creepy still played at the back of my mind.

A pot lid clanged in the background. "I have a feeling you'd appreciate it if I trucked this meal over to your kitchen later this afternoon. You don't sound in good enough shape to make it safely to my back door."

"Nonsense. Promise to feed me, and I can make it across the Gobi Desert in a sandstorm."

"See you at five, then. Unless you get a better offer."

"Like what?" I asked. "Leftover funeral luncheon sandwiches? Dinner at the bottom of a quarry with Alvin? An evening up at Camp David with the president?"

"I had a fast food meal with a certain state trooper in mind."

Thinking of the state trooper made me salivate, but not for fast food. "I saw him last night at the funeral home."

"What did he want there?"

"I'll tell you all about it over dinner," I promised.

"Hm. As tired as you sound, I'll be lucky if you can remember who you buried today, let alone what happened with Officer Hunk last night."

"Believe me, I may feel as if a dozen elephants marched over me in my sleep, but no way could I forget burying Nancy. Remind me to tell you about the luncheon, too."

"Real fun time, huh?"

"Not for John Huff."

We said goodbye. I marched into my office and dug out my materials for the next church newsletter. I checked the calendar. The month ahead looked like my busiest yet as pastor at St. Luke's. The children's pageant, the church Christmas party, the choir banquet (my suggestion they change it to an Epiphany banquet so they could schedule it in the nearly empty January agenda met with the grand cry of all church objections: "We've always done it this way"), the Hanging of the Greens, the Christmas services.

Throw in finding a body in the sacristy to start the season and you have a truly awful Advent. Worry about John chewed a raw spot at the back of my brain. Maybe the busyness of the month would help me put that aside. After all, what more could I do to help him? With Nancy buried, I could only visit him and provide a listening ear while he expressed his grief. Then the reality of visiting John in jail hit me.

This time the ringing of the phone came as an escape from my thoughts.

"Pastor Abby, it's John Huff. I'm calling from the jail

in Frederick. They've arrested me for Nancy's murder. I called my son and asked him to get me a lawyer. He refused. He said the cops told him things that convinced him I killed her. Pastor, someone is out to get me. I don't have anywhere to turn but you."

Chapter Seven

Only by reminding myself that I couldn't afford to pay a speeding ticket if I wanted to finish my Christmas shopping this week did I manage to stay near the speed limit on my way into Frederick. I'd called my neighbor and canceled our supper together. Dora had promised to save me some soup at any hour I wanted. We both figured this run would take most of the evening.

But we had miscalculated. John hadn't anything more to tell me than he'd already said over the phone. His speculation that the police wanted to frame him appeared to come from overhearing parts of conversations during his processing at the jail. I made some calls for John. No answer at Bill and Suzie's, but his brother agreed immediately to talk to some bondsmen about putting up a bond if the judge granted him bail at his arraignment.

I tried unsuccessfully to get in contact with Trooper Eichelberger, too, though I had to admit I didn't know exactly why. He hadn't been with officers who'd arrested John, and he had already indicated he couldn't provide me with any information about the case. What would I do with it anyway?

Since I had come all the way into Frederick, I hit the mall and attempted to pare my Christmas shopping list down to the last few items. Naturally the perfect item my mother couldn't possibly complain about this time had sold out two hours before I got there. When the store offered to place a special order but couldn't guarantee delivery by Christmas, I declined.

With my spirits only slightly less dark than the December evening, I headed back toward Thurmont. On an impulse, I drove by Bill and Suzie's home. Lights burned in the living room, so I parked at the curb and rang the bell.

Suzie answered the door in her robe. The expression on her face when she saw me indicated surprise but not pleasure.

"Come in, Pastor Abby. I hope you're not here to bawl Bill out for his behavior today. Not that I'm proud of it myself, but it won't do any good. He's not here."

"Actually, that's not my style. But I had hoped to appeal to him to put aside some of his bad feelings toward his father. John really needs him right now."

We walked into the kitchen where Bill had revealed his reasons for suspecting his father of his mother's murder. Unlike the previous time, neatness did not reign. Dirty dishes cluttered the counter. Suzie's hair sat scrunched on one side of her head and puffed out like Bozo's on the other.

"Give him a couple of days. The funeral, especially watching that box go into the ground with his mom's body in it, hit him hard. I think he interpreted his dad's remoteness as guilt." She pulled the robe tighter around her neck and checked the buttons, then glanced anxiously at the sink as if she expected me to make some comment about her unfinished housework.

"This afternoon's *Frederick News* reported that a witness saw John in town on Sunday morning, so I suspect he anticipated the arrest on Friday."

Suzie's eyebrows shot up under the stray locks of hair. "He may have expected to get arrested ever since last Sunday."

"So you agree with Bill. You also think John's guilty."

Suzie rose from the table and began to place the dishes from the counter into the dishwasher. "Maybe. I don't know what to think. I'm afraid to think."

I waited a beat and then quietly asked, "What about this scares you?"

She dropped a pan into the sink with a clang, squirted it with detergent, and ran some water into it. "Things like this don't exactly help a marriage."

"No, I suppose not." I waited.

"The best thing we can do, including you, Pastor, is to let matters run their course."

"Suzie, I know that Nancy had lunch several times with someone up in Gettysburg."

She stared at me in silence.

"I know your father met her there."

She swallowed and had to try twice before she could get the next words out of her mouth. "Do the police know?"

"Not from me, but if I found this out, they'll know soon if they don't now."

"My dad told me about it. They just had lunch together. His loneliness since my mother died has practically driven him crazy. But he didn't kill her. Why would he? She took an interest in him."

"Your father-in-law thought some sort of relationship existed, though he didn't know what kind. He suspected the worst."

She straightened her back. "Well, that supports the likelihood that he killed Nancy."

"I'm sure the police will agree with you."

"But you don't."

"No, I don't. John insists he didn't kill her, and I believe him."

Her eyes narrowed, and she sat down at the table again. "Enough to try to pin the murder on someone else. On *my* father."

"Suzie, I'm not the police. I'm not trying to pin anything

on anyone. John needs his family right now. That's my role in this. Taking care of him, and of you and Bill, too."

"We appreciate your concern," she said in a tone that meant "Butt out."

"Thank you." Two could play that game.

"Bill went to a basketball game down in Washington. I must have fallen asleep waiting up for him."

"Ask him to call me in the morning. I'm not expecting miracles, Suzie, but a family needs to stand together at times like this."

She nodded. "I don't know what to do about any of this. About Bill's feelings or my dad's involvement. After Nancy's murder, I got so scared John would find out about my father and kill him, too. If he did kill Bill's mom, I mean. Maybe he didn't. I don't pretend to feel as strongly about it as Bill does."

Or maybe she knew, or feared she knew, who had murdered her mother-in-law.

When I got home and shed my ministerial outfit, I donned my warmest sweatsuit and invaded the kitchen.

Not that this did me any good. I had forgotten to include the supermarket in my shopping spree, and my cupboards looked emptier than Orioles Park at Camden Yards on New Year's Day. When I heard the knock on my back door, I hurried to welcome my rescuer.

"About time you got home," Dora complained. "Good thing this soup heats up fast. God definitely had you in mind when he let humankind invent the microwave."

"Why should I learn to cook with you next door? Your food tastes better than anything I'd concoct."

"Sit down and let me get some of this ready for both of us. I went light on supper, figuring you'd never get around to eating while you were gallivanting around Frederick. What took you so long? Did they decide at the jail you looked suspicious and they'd better hang on to you for a while?"

I grabbed two large soup bowls from the cabinet over the dishwasher. Dora had already pulled spoons from the silverware drawer and napkins from the holder near the back of the stove.

She waved one of the napkins at me. "Pumpkins and witches? We passed Halloween over a month ago."

"I got a really good deal on those napkins the first of November. I'll put them away for Christmas."

Dora closed her eyes and shook her head slowly to show her disbelief at my lack of proper standards. "You'll probably have the Christmas ones still out at Easter."

"Only if I get as good a deal on them as I did on the Halloween ones."

A few minutes later, I took my first sip of the divine brew and felt every muscle in my body relax as if seven certified massage therapists were working on me at the same time.

"How'd things go in Frederick?"

"John's brother's going to arrange a bond for him. Probably a waste of time, given the charge. I'm guessing the judge won't grant bail."

"Don't see why not. He's hardly a threat to flee the country. Unless it's elk hunting season in Canada."

The mention of hunting made me think of Alvin. "Do you have any wisdom to share about handling Alvin Porter and his campaign against me?"

"If Ike Eichelberger would just get on the stick and come through with a diamond ring, your worries about Alvin would disappear."

"Hey, I haven't even had a date with this fellow, and you've got me marching down the aisle to 'Trumpet Voluntary.' I don't even know if he's married or engaged or heavily involved with someone."

"He's not. I checked. Tell me you wouldn't look great

in a white gown, placing your hand in his, standing on the other side of the service book for a change." She passed out dessert.

"Seriously, Dora, who else can I talk to who might shed some light on Nancy's murder?"

She halted a forkful of cherry cobbler halfway between her plate and her mouth. "Let the cops do that. You have your hands full enough with St. Luke's."

"True, but I can't desert John the way most of his family has. I might find something out that would help clear him. Something the police could use to find the real killer."

"Could be they already have."

Now I took a turn freezing a glob of cobbler in midair. "That just doesn't ring true."

"Sometimes the obvious person is the culprit, you know," Dora warned.

"Do you really think he's guilty?"

She stared into my eyes for a full minute, then put her fork down. "Not if you don't."

"What do you think of Frank Teller as a possible murderer?" I asked.

"Why would he kill her? Obviously he got something out of their relationship, or he wouldn't have continued it."

"Suzie seems worried that he's next in line if the authorities cross John off as a suspect."

"Maybe she'd better worry about herself. The cops might figure she could have done her mother-in-law in to protect her father. Not to mention ridding herself of a real annoyance."

That had crossed my mind, too. I wondered if Officer Eichelberger had found out where Suzie and John were early Sunday morning. On the other hand, they'd no doubt provide an alibi for one another.

I knew Dora had given me good advice, to leave the whole business of John's guilt or innocence to the legal system. But I couldn't let go that easily. With John depending on me, I knew I would still dig for more information about Nancy and her death. When Alvin had gone on the attack in the past, John had defended me more than once. I had to hope I wouldn't make things worse for him.

Despite my best efforts, I couldn't make myself sleep in the next morning. My mind jumped from John's tribulations to Alvin's plans to sack me to the six million meetings and events scheduled at the church that I didn't dare miss. At least some of my inquiries on John's behalf also fell into the category of funeral follow-up/grief counseling.

The brilliant idea of questioning Nancy's mother popped into my mind. Perhaps the late Mrs. Huff had confided things to her mom that she hadn't told anyone else. Who would have more of an interest in exposing her daughter's killer? As soon as I had breakfast, I drove to Emmitsburg and knocked on the door of the grieving parent.

My reception there made the conversation with Suzie the evening before seem positively cozy. She opened the door and immediately said, "Oh, I know you. You're the one ruining that church my daughter tried so hard to keep on the straight and narrow. If you had any concern for the safety of your members, that nutty husband of hers couldn't have gotten in and murdered her."

When all else fails, hook them by identifying with their problems. "This week has been very trying for you," I said. "Could I come in and talk with you about it and about Nancy?"

"I saw the way you fawned all over the creep yesterday at the luncheon. He's too old for you. Of course, maybe you *want* old and useless—just your type."

Ah, evidence of Alvin's work. "Your daughter served our congregation faithfully, and we'll miss her careful attention to detail and her constant energy."

"You already went over that in your sermon yesterday.

Rotten funeral, by the way. Worst I've ever attended. Best you can do, I suppose."

Gentle and comforting hadn't worked. Maybe an appeal to vengeance would. "I'm sure you don't want her killer to go unpunished. Suppose John's not the one. Can you tell me anything she mentioned that might point to someone else?"

"Nancy had to put up with you because she went to St. Luke's, but I don't have to."

The door slammed in my face. *Yeah, Abby, you really hooked that one.*

At least I could count on a more pleasant greeting at my next stop. I numbered Phyllis Huff, John's mother, among the sweetest individuals God ever placed on earth, though Nancy hadn't shared that assessment. In her worst moods, Nancy had called Phyllis "the old battleaxe" or "the Wicked Witch of the Woods" because her house was down a narrow lane lined with old maples and locust trees.

The front door swung open before I had a chance to lock my car. "Come on in, Pastor," Phyllis greeted me. "I didn't get a chance to tell you what a lovely service you had for Nancy yesterday. Our family appreciated it so much. And we can't thank you enough for the way you've been there for John."

"I want to do anything I can to help all of you through this terrible time."

"I'd like to grab my grandson and give him a good shake, but I suppose we each have to grieve in our own way." She led me into her living room and motioned for me to choose a place to sit. Then she disappeared down the hallway into her kitchen.

Phyllis reminded me of my own grandmother, and that probably explained the level of comfort I always felt in her home. A Victorian sideboard stood guard in the dining room just beyond a rectangular archway framed in walnut woodwork. The comfy couch and armchairs had colorful afghans draped over their backs, and photographs of her sons' families ruled the mantel and walls.

"I just made tea." She handed me a delicate hand-painted cup. "It's still hot. I'm afraid I ate all the cookies, though. Shouldn't at my age, but we all have to have one vice to keep us humble. My sweet tooth's mine."

I took a sip of the dark beverage and felt a warmth like love radiate outward from the center of my body. "You're a doll, Phyllis. I drove up to see Nancy's mother before I came here. I didn't get as warm a welcome, though."

"I imagine you didn't. Nancy came by her disposition honestly." My hostess blushed. "How unkind of me to speak ill of the dead, not to mention of my own daughter-in-law. Please excuse my rudeness, Pastor."

This woman had to know what sorts of names her son's wife had occasionally called her. The disparity of generosity people showed in assessing other individuals never ceased to amaze me.

"John seems worried the police will stop looking for Nancy's killer because they've arrested their most obvious candidate," I said. "Can you help me think of people who might have had a reason to kill her?"

"People may have excuses, but does anyone ever have a valid reason for murdering someone?" A single tear slid down the deep crease beside her nose. "I don't mean self-defense, of course. And I imagine I would feel differently about someone who'd harmed my child."

"Nancy had a talent for ruffling people's feathers. Who disliked her the most?"

I could see the old woman struggle between her desire to help out her son and her determination to avoid bashing her late daughter-in-law.

"John told me she'd lost one of her best friends in a business deal gone bad," Phyllis admitted. That had to be Charlotte Baker's planned crafts store. "You know how she talked about people. She didn't like the ones she worked with, except for her boss, Mr. Briggs. She thought he could walk on water."

She picked up a photo from the end table near her chair. A much younger John, Nancy, and Bill, who couldn't have been older than twelve, looked out from a campsite on a lake.

"She talked so mean about that judge she used to work for," Phyllis continued. "But a man in his position could certainly afford to ignore her. Who would listen to her instead of him?"

"Her manner seemed to bother Celia more than Tom." While Tom had supplied stories about Nancy, Celia hadn't responded.

She straightened in her chair. "Tom Martin. Yes, that's his name. I couldn't remember it. I always suspected he got rid of her because he didn't want to put up with her any longer, and she never forgot a slight."

Imagined or real, if I knew Nancy, but I kept that to myself.

Phyllis put back the photograph and frowned. "She also told me about two weeks ago that she intended to do her best to get our organist fired. She'd informed him of her plan, hoping he'd resign and save her the trouble."

"They didn't get along well. Still, I find it hard to believe she could worry him enough or make him angry enough to kill her."

She sighed. "You're probably right. Warren's temper flashes pretty quickly, from what I've seen, but he mostly seems able to ignore her or pay her back in kind. He picked at her constantly after she lambasted him during choir practice. She quit the choir in retaliation, which I figure was exactly what he hoped for."

"I know John and Nancy were going through a particularly difficult time in their marriage."

She pursed her lips and jiggled the glasses resting on the bridge of her nose. "You mean Frank Teller."

I almost dropped the antique teacup and needed a quick swoop with my free hand to save it from disaster.

"You . . . you know about him?"

"Oh, my, yes. One of my so-called longtime friends called me up weeks ago and gave me an earful. She wanted me to rush over to John's and tell him all about it. I figured they had enough problems without adding harmful gossip to the mix. Besides, who knows the truth about that? Maybe I don't even want to."

"Could he have had a reason to murder Nancy?"

Phyllis threw up her hands in supplication to the powers above. "Who knows? I think the only time I ever met the man was at Bill and Suzie's wedding."

She'd covered the same list of potential suspects I'd generated in my daybook at home. Minus her grandson and his wife, naturally. Pleasant as it was, talking to Phyllis hadn't generated any new avenues for me to explore in helping John's defense.

After a brief prayer, I thanked her for the tea and the conversation and excused myself. She stopped me in the open doorway and hugged me.

"Be careful, Pastor Abby," she said. "Don't put yourself in danger trying to help my son."

Chapter Eight

When I arrived home, I checked my answering machine to see if Bill had called. Suzie had asked me to give him some time. Maybe saving my pestering for later made sense, but I didn't plan to give up on him.

Then again, perhaps he had other reasons for his attitude, and for not calling. Pointing the finger at his father effectively removed his wife and her father from scrutiny. And himself, too. But could I really imagine Bill had killed his own mother? Silly to say it, but he didn't seem the type. Protecting someone else fit his character better, but his conviction about his dad's guilt appeared sincere. In spite of that, I couldn't cross him off my list.

I scrutinized my calendar and gulped when I compared the number of shut-ins on my "to visit" list with the number of days left before Christmas. After circling the names of three elderly members who lived close together, I grabbed my handy-dandy communion kit (an embroidered craft box I'd converted for this purpose) and hit the road.

Usually I called ahead to make sure the individuals on my schedule plan to be home, but I estimated my chances to find them in today as pretty good.

I thought wrong. Two of my three targeted chickens had flown the coop. Amazing how easily conditions could shut people into their houses with regard to church attendance, but the mall had strange restorative powers. I saw people there who swore they couldn't manage to negotiate the walkway from the parking lot to the church door.

Inspiration struck. With John sitting in jail, Frank Teller had to feel off the hook. Suzie could easily call him and tell him she thought I had a campaign going to blame him for Nancy's death. My odds of talking to him before she did decreased every hour.

The phone book supplied his address. Should I call ahead? No. He might refuse to see me or see the call as a warning and take off someplace I couldn't find him. Besides, I couldn't think of a valid reason I could give him for coming to his house other than to help John. While I couldn't expect him to advocate John's release at his own expense, he offered a source of information about Nancy quite different from the ones I'd already mined.

How bad could this turn out? I'd survived my attempt to talk to Nancy's mother. As difficult as a conversation with Frank promised to be, I could make it through this, too.

Frank looked confused when he answered his door. Confused over finding me familiar but not identifiable? Uncertain over what I wanted? Nervous about what he could say to get rid of me without giving away any information he didn't want me to know? All of the above?

"Hello, Mr. Teller. I'm Pastor Abby Shaw from St. Luke's. I'd like to talk to you about Nancy Huff."

He nodded and wet his lips. "Sure. You did her funeral. Come on in."

His living room astonished me. I'd never seen so many ruffles in one space. Obviously he hadn't redecorated after his wife's death, and the late Mrs. Teller must have had a strong determination to make her home as feminine as possible. The pale blue rug suited the pink couch and matching armchairs with their pattern of tiny white roses. About a thousand lace-covered throw pillows in various pastel shades defended the furniture against all comers. The burly widower was discordant with his setting.

I took the chair nearest the door in case I needed to beat a hasty retreat. "I'm sure you know the state police arrested John Huff yesterday."

He shoved a few lace cushions to one side and sat on the couch. "Yes, Suzie called me and told me. Have to admit it took me by surprise. He doesn't seem the type. Wouldn't have thought he had it in him to be that decisive, to be honest."

"I'm convinced he didn't kill his wife."

"And you need to talk to me about that because . . . ?" He made circles in the air in front of him to encourage me to get to my point.

"Mr. Teller, I know that you and Nancy had a relationship."

"Frank. I'm only Mr. Teller to the men I boss and when I go to the bank to ask for a loan. Call me Frank. Now about me and Nancy. You call what we had a friendship. Nothing more."

"I didn't intend to suggest anything else." Actually, I did, but I didn't want to create a confrontation over that. "If John is innocent, then someone else murdered Nancy. Since you knew her better than I did, I thought you might have some ideas about who would want to cause her harm."

He picked up one of the small pillows and squeezed it in his fist. "Look, I liked Nancy. We made good sounding boards for each other. But that doesn't mean I didn't see her faults. To me, she was gentle, a good listener, somebody who'd encourage me to crawl out of my shell but wouldn't put up with any of my garbage. To people she didn't like, she could be a real harpy. I don't kid myself for a minute that she was easy to work with or live with."

I leaned forward. My fingers itched to get into my purse and pull out my notepad, but I didn't want to destroy the flow of information.

"So you and Nancy shared an occasional lunch and acted as confidants for one another. That means she probably told you things she didn't tell anyone else."

"I want to make sure you understand we didn't share anything more than lunch and some personal conversation." His eyes flashed a warning to step lightly.

"Frank, I don't have any reason to doubt you." Okay, the natural human inclination was to disbelieve protestations of innocence, but I had information gathering on my agenda, not gossip or censure. "Did she name anyone who had threatened her? Or anyone who held a grudge against her?" I hoped I'd kept some of the eagerness I felt out of my voice.

"Threats? None I know of." He glanced over to the family portrait on the far wall. "Grudges? Well, a number of people had a reason to hold a grudge. For instance, she didn't exactly make my daughter's hit parade."

"Can you give me some names of people who'd fall into that category?" Now my fingertips really did itch for a pen and paper.

"She told Warren Weston she planned to get him dismissed. He told her she'd fry in hell before he'd let her rob him of his position."

That certainly upped the ante for Warren's status as a potential culprit.

"Anyone else?"

He regarded me silently for a moment. "Pastor, the police have investigated this whole business. I doubt if they've finished. Why don't you let them do their job, and you stick to yours?"

My personal theme song for the month had begun to form. The lyrics ran something like this:

> Keep your nose to yourself,
> Just do your work.

If you don't listen,
You're a pain and a jerk.

The music hadn't settled yet, but what I heard so far was in a minor key.

"I'm sure you're right." I smiled my most conciliatory smile. "I guess I've hoped to find some crumb of information the police don't have yet that might help John, might help expose the real killer."

"You have a list of suspects they should look into?" His narrowed eyes warned me not to give the wrong answer to this question.

"Not really. Like you, I know of some people who'd gotten mad at Nancy, but no one who seemed angry enough to want her dead." No way would I give him my list of possible perpetrators. Frank appeared to be a nice enough guy, but his self-interest might come into play in a major way.

He wrapped a hand around his chin and shook his head. "If John really thought Nancy and I had an affair going, he'd have had the most reason of anyone. He had to live with her day in and day out, too. I heard he came to Thurmont early Sunday and then left again, but he didn't tell the cops about it. That has to count against him."

Obviously it had; the man was in jail. No need to ask how Frank had heard about John's dawn visit. By now both newspapers and at least three radio stations had reported this tidbit.

"On the other hand, I feel certain John didn't know about you and Nancy. He suspected she, uh, was seeing someone, but he didn't know who."

Given Frank's frown, I decided to change the subject quickly. "Bill seems so convinced his father's the murderer. Doesn't that puzzle you?" I asked.

"Don't tell me you think Bill could have done it." His

expression mirrored the horror in his voice. "She was his mother, for cripes sake!"

Joan Crawford, Lucrezia Borgia, and Medusa were mothers too, but I didn't intend to point that out to Frank.

"No, no, of course not. I simply can't believe how quickly everyone has dropped the hunt for Nancy's killer. Even if John did come back to town on Sunday and then hide the fact, he and Nancy had survived troubles between them before. To me, the evidence doesn't add up to a compelling argument for his guilt. I hate the idea of Nancy's murderer going free."

"What's your special interest in John Huff?" he said.

Gee, what kind of signals was I giving off that people kept jumping to the same conclusion about my desperation for a man? "The connection to St. Luke's. And a sense that John doesn't have very many people on his side."

Frank eased himself up from the sofa, knocking the throw pillows back into place with one hand as he rose. "Tell you what, Pastor. If I think of anything Nancy said that could possibly, even by the greatest stretch of my imagination, implicate anyone other than John in her death, I'll call the cops and tell them about it. But I won't call you. You should go home and get back to your church work. Leave the detecting to the detectives."

Ah, the sweet strains of my theme song again, signaling the end of another episode in my search for evidence to help John Huff. I stood up at this cue.

"Thanks for seeing me. You and Nancy apparently had a special friendship, and I know you will miss her."

He didn't respond except to nod and open the door for me to leave.

Searching under the furniture for clerical collar tabs took me a mere twelve minutes on Sunday morning and netted me half a dozen of the little plastic devils. Now I could face the Second Sunday in Advent at St. Luke's. Unless the roof fell in or the boiler blew up in the middle of the service, today would have to be an improvement over the previous Sunday. I even found a pair of pantyhose without runs or holes on only the second try.

The quiet church gave me the creeps for the first few minutes after I entered. Normally I enjoyed that time. It gave me a chance to get my things in order for the service and the rest of the morning. Today I felt edgy. I berated myself. What could happen? Did I have some weird idea crawling around in my cranium that a serial killer had decided to stalk St. Luke's, exterminating whomever arrived at the church first?

Barb Johnson appeared in my office a few minutes before Sunday School opened. "Have you seen the crowds today? This place is really hopping."

"I guess Nancy's death put us on the map. Thinking of St. Luke's service as an object of rubbernecking like some bloody accident out on Route 15 doesn't thrill me." I shuddered.

"Well, that no doubt has led to part of today's action. But the other thing has played a big role, too." She looked at me expectantly.

"The other thing?"

"With the funeral and John and all, you must have missed the fact that a lot of people are hot under the collar and ready to rumble."

"Over something I did?" How like a pastor to assume I had caused the dissatisfaction.

"No, but you know how it goes. Someone who comes out on the losing end of the debate will have a bitter word or two for you for not taking their side." She threw up her hands in mock surrender. "You've forgotten what else we've scheduled for today, haven't you?" She put a sympathetic hand on my shoulder and pointed toward the huge calendar visible in the secretary's office on the other side of the doorway.

How could I have forgotten? The large red letters screamed, "CHRISTMAS TREE DECISION MEETING!" Barb had warned me that groups had formed to defend their idea of what the St. Luke's Christmas tree should look like. I hadn't realized that last year's tree had departed from previous practices, setting up warring camps wanting either more changes or a return to the prior status.

With visions of angry parishioners chucking hymnals at one another and ripping the pews from the floor to form barricades, I floated somnolently through Sunday School and the service. Aside from one point during the sermon where I lost my train of thought and played for a moment with declaring a weeklong intermission (Advent is a time of waiting, after all), I survived in relatively good shape. My inner radar signaled I wouldn't come out of the rest of the day so easily.

After the recessional and dismissal, the majority of the congregation moved to the fellowship hall for the Great Debate. Motioning wildly for me to come sit beside him, Alvin Porter tried valiantly to get my attention before the meeting began. But members asking after John and his family cornered me and saved me from a fate worse than Alvin. Frank Teller was sitting right behind Alvin and giving him an earful.

When a large number of speakers had expressed their opinions about the tree, the predictable result occurred: Warren promised the worship and music committee would consider their input and make a recommendation to the board.

Several people came up to me to remind me of upcoming events or make one last plea for their tree preference. I felt a heavy paw on my shoulder and spun around to face Alvin.

"Well, Pastor," he said, making the word sound like a reprimand, "you've done it now. We need to talk, and we need to talk this very minute."

Chapter Nine

"Gee, Alvin," I said, "I'd like nothing better than to talk to you, but I'm already late for an appointment." With my lunch.

He grabbed my arm just above the elbow and squeezed. "I'm the president of the board, and your appointment will have to wait. What I have to say won't keep." He squeezed harder.

I pasted on my I'm-being-pleasant smile. "If you don't let go of me this second, I am going to scream with pain, slump to the floor, and throw a fit."

He dropped my arm as if it had burned him. "No reason to make this any more unpleasant than necessary."

"Remember that while we're talking. Let's go to my office."

His hand twitched as if he could barely restrain himself from grabbing me again, but he nodded and followed me down the hall.

"Perhaps we should invite Barb to join us, as vice president of the board," I said.

Mottles appeared on his face. "What I have to say has nothing to do with Barb. And you can forget trying to get someone else in here to act as your defender. You've gotten yourself into this trouble all on your own."

I sat down in my throne-like office chair and motioned to him to take either of the other chairs. "Interesting tie."

I hoped the fashion diversion and my death grip on the chair arms would hide the quaking I felt under my skin.

He looked down at the hunting dogs dragging dead pheasants out of tall grass. Where did he get these things? I never saw anything like them in the department stores in Frederick. Did some company publish a catalog called *Weird and Repulsive Ties*? "Marsha likes it, too. She says it brings out the color of my eyes."

"I see what she means." The red and yellow both showed up better with the aid of this accessory.

"I've gotten complaints that you're running around the county talking to people." His glare dared me to deny the accusation.

"How strange. Usually I hear that I don't visit enough. I have tried to get ahead on my shut-in home calls this month. With the holidays coming—"

"Skip the excuses. You know full well what I mean." Alvin's eyes closed into little pig-like slits. "You haven't done church visits. You've spent your time playing cop. People are tired of you bothering them. They resent your implications that they had something to do with Nancy's death."

"People like Frank Teller."

Alvin slid the knot on his tie higher, forcing one retriever out of sight and leaving the pheasant hanging in space. "I've heard the same complaint from several sources. The names aren't the issue. Your behavior is the issue. We hired you to serve as our pastor, not to play policewoman."

I gripped the arms of my chair and felt the slickness of the leather. "I suppose you'd prefer John Huff to go to prison even if he's innocent."

His nostrils flared. "I *suppose* you'd better stick to your job and let the authorities handle the murder investigation. How ridiculous of you to think you can find out something they can't. You mess up enough things at St. Luke's without exercising your talent for ruination across the community, too."

I felt my cheeks color. "I've stopped in to see some people as part of my pastoral duties. In spite of what you seem to think, I work very hard to care for St. Luke's members. Yes, I admit I hoped some evidence would turn up that might convince the police to take a good look at people other than John. Someone killed Nancy, and I don't think John's the one. But I've spent the majority of my time and effort on my regular parish work."

Alvin tilted his head back and pointed his bulbous nose at me. "We don't pay you for the majority of your time. We pay you for all of it. If I hear we're getting less than that, you can bet your clerical collar I'll do everything in my power to get you dismissed."

I felt my hair frizzing from the steam rising off my neck. "Including expanding your current campaign of vicious rumors, I assume."

The blotches on Alvin's face disappeared into a generalized redness. His shirt tightened around his neck. "I have no idea what you mean."

"Oh, I think you do. I know that pastors rarely sue members of their congregation for slander, but I'll bet it has happened."

He snorted. "Are you threatening me?"

"I'm informing you that I won't sit by and let you sandbag me. I've fulfilled my role as the pastor of St. Luke's, and I'll continue to do that to the best of my ability."

"That's the problem. Your best doesn't come up to a high enough standard." His lips rolled back from his teeth, exposing teeth the color of the golden retrievers on his tie.

"So you say, but not everyone shares your opinion. You've had your say, Mr. Porter. This conversation is over."

He turned even redder. "You're dismissing me?"

I stood and reached for my coat, hoping he couldn't see

the shaking I felt inside. "Stay as long as you like. I have things to do. I'm leaving. Goodbye."

I parked the car in the garage, went straight to my bedroom, pulled down the shades, crawled under the covers, and hid in the dark.

But my mind wouldn't turn off and let me sleep. Thoughts kept creeping past my determination to push them away. I wanted to slap Alvin Porter. I wanted to slap Frank Teller and anyone else who had ratted on me to Alvin. Most of all, I wanted to slap myself silly for getting into such a horrible position without helping John one iota.

At that thought, visions of Greek letters began to dance in my head. Oh, great. It couldn't be sugarplums, it had to be letters pirouetting behind my eyelids. I hummed some appropriate music for their performance. The omegas seemed to twirl the fastest. Last letter of that alphabet. A sign my career would soon come to an end? I pulled the duvet over my head.

When I wriggled out from my hiding place, the sun had already begun to set. My stomach reminded me that I still hadn't made a run to the supermarket. I glanced across the lawn at Dora's house, wondering if I could plead a pity supper out of her again. The house stood dark under the bare maple branches that shaded it in the summer.

I struggled into jeans and a sweatshirt and headed for Thurmont. First I'd pick up a burger so I didn't pile the grocery store's entire stash of junk food into my cart as I sailed up and down the supermarket aisles. As tiny pieces of ice pelted the windshield, I parked under the welcoming glow of the fast food sign and ran into the restaurant.

My teeth had sunk through the bun but hadn't yet reached the meat when I felt a hand on my shoulder. I jumped to my feet, dropping my sandwich. The burger landed on its side and started to roll across the table.

Trooper Eichelberger grabbed it just before it plunged

off the edge and onto the floor. "Your burger, ma'am." He held it out toward me.

I lifted the bun and slid my errant meat patty back into its rightful place. "You practically scared me into January."

"The noise level gets a little high in here this time of day, and I thought you might not hear me if I asked, so I touched your shoulder to get your attention." In spite of his obvious efforts, he broke into a grin the size of Catoctin Mountain, visible behind us through the restaurant's windows.

"Asked me what?" I attributed my continuing shaking mostly to tiredness and my little talk with Alvin.

"If you'd mind some company while you eat. Unless you had plans to use that sandwich for Frisbee practice instead of a meal."

"This hasn't been my best week as a pastor. Maybe I should consider a switch to professional athlete."

As he sipped his milkshake, he looked me up and down with a glance that suggested Dora might be right about his appraisal of me. "That depends. How good's your throwing arm?"

"Well, so far the Orioles haven't offered me a huge signing bonus to join their bullpen. Guess I'll have to stay with what I'm doing."

He slurped the last drips of shake through his straw. When I did that, I sounded like an industrial-strength vacuum cleaner sucking up sand. How did he manage to make even that sound cute?

His eyebrows jiggled. "This a bad time of year for ministers?"

"Generally not the best. People have such high expectations for the holidays, and reality doesn't often live up to those."

"Bad time for my line of work, too. For a lot of the same reasons." He scrunched the cup in one hand and tossed it into the nearby garbage bin. "Tough week, aside from Mrs. Huff's burial?"

I swallowed the bite of cheeseburger in my mouth. "We had a rough meeting today, with half the congregation threatening to go to war over the Christmas tree."

"The real or fake debate?"

"You name it. Proper type, proper size, proper lights, proper decorations. About the only thing that didn't come up for discussion was the color of the tree."

"Sounds like we both need a chance to escape. What would you say to joining me for a movie in Frederick this evening?"

I dropped what remained of my burger onto my lap. "I'd like that better than a raise. But I have to work. We have a practice for the church's Christmas pageant tonight."

"Will a good time be had by all?" His freckles danced under the florescent lights. Sure beat dancing letters from the Greek alphabet.

"Oh, sure. This will provide a little more amusement than a train wreck. Trooper Eichelberger, I really want to accept your invitation. If I thought I could miss this meeting without getting into deeper trouble, I would. Do you give rain checks?"

"Can't schedule another time for a movie right now because I don't know my schedule past Tuesday. I'll give you a call when I have a better idea of my free time. But what do you mean about getting into trouble?" His frown scrunched the freckles into little bunches. Gosh, freckles that prominent in December.

I gulped. I couldn't lie. Not only could I not lie to a cop, I couldn't lie to someone who had invited me to a movie. If this was the start of a relationship, I didn't want to begin with a fib.

"As a pastor, I stop in to see a lot of people. Mostly shut-ins, but other people, too." I hesitated.

He leaned his chair back on two legs and stuck his hands

in his pockets. "Let me guess. To try to help out John Huff, you've asked some fairly nosy questions. Someone took exception to that, and then—well, then what happened?"

"You know who Frank Teller is." I looked at him to see if he understood my implication.

"Yeah. Nancy's good friend and lunch buddy." He scratched his jaw where a five o'clock shadow had begun to appear.

"He doesn't belong to St. Luke's, but he showed up for the Christmas tree discussion, sat behind the board president, and gave him an earful. Apparently another individual or two got to our slimy executive as well. After the meeting, the president told me to stick to my pastoral duties and stop playing detective, or he'll see I get fired."

The blond eyebrows shot up. "Can he do that?"

"Not directly. But he's already started some rumors he hopes will get the bishop to remove me."

"Rumors?"

"He's telling people Mrs. Miller's daughter claims I've never visited her mother. Mrs. Miller has Alzheimer's; she thinks I'm her cousin Shirley from Milwaukee."

"Maybe Alvin just can't handle having a foxy pastor."

I felt the blood color my skin from my neck to my scalp.

He laughed at my discomfort. "Pastor Shaw—can I call you Abby?" He wiped the moisture from the corner of his right eye.

"Please do. What should I call you? What does the E. stand for?"

With a sly grin on his face, he shook his head. "It's just an initial. I'm Ike."

"Come on, you can tell me. I won't spread it around." I made fluttering "move forward" motions with the fingers of both hands.

"No way."

"All right then, give me some professional advice."

"Glad to. Don't drive more than five miles over the limit."

I threw my balled-up burger wrapper at him. He caught it and clipped me on the nose with it. "I'm serious," I said. "How much trouble can I get into trying to dig up evidence that points to someone other than John Huff?"

He twisted the paper wrapper from my straw and tied it into a knot. "Depends on how mad you make the people you're asking questions. With your occupation, you're pretty free to visit people. Sort of right up your vocational alley, right?"

My head bobbed.

"Not much worse than a door slammed in your face seems likely. Of course, you've mentioned this board president who has a scheme going to dump you. I guess you could throw fuel on that fire. Particularly if he can make it look like you're doing this instead of your church work."

He'd hit on exactly what Alvin planned to do. I'd have to cut my visits back to members only. That made me mad. I hadn't neglected my work, though I had enlarged its scope a little. Hadn't stupid Alvin ever heard of outreach in the community?

"One other thing you may not have thought of." Ike laid his large hand over mine. I felt as if I had a heated glove on. "If you happen to be right that someone else killed Nancy, you could make that person very nervous."

"You mean the murderer might want to eliminate me to prevent exposure." I found my hand grasping his from beneath.

He gave my fingers a comforting squeeze. "Yeah. If you uncover anything significant, even a small detail, call the state police barracks or get ahold of me."

"I have to go," I said. "My refrigerator's empty, and a person can only stand so many peanut butter and relish sandwiches. I have to rush through the supermarket because I can't afford to sail into the pageant practice late."

The freckles all collected around his nose as he screwed up his facial muscles. "Yuck. Peanut butter and relish? What ever happened to strawberry preserves? Not against your religion, are they?"

"I ran out and had to make do."

He stood up and zipped up his parka. "You win points for creativity for that menu item, if not for culinary genius."

As he pushed open the door, he stopped and looked back at me. "The E? My parents wanted a girl, so they named me Ellen." He winked and stepped out into the shower of sleet.

When I arrived at St. Luke's, cars already filled the parking lot. I parked on one of the cemetery roads and made my way through the cold rain flecked with snowflakes. At least the sleet had stopped, so the families attending the pageant practice could travel home more safely. The lights beckoned from the hall windows, but I wondered if I would find as welcome a reception once I got inside.

Joan Kress, our Sunday School superintendent, prompted the groups of children to shout out their pieces. Most of them continued to whisper, making their performances inaudible over the conversations of the waiting and admiring parents.

Alvin shot darts at me with his eyes through the whole proceedings. Barb Johnson leaned over and tapped my arm. "Boy, the prez looks loaded for bear," she said. "What's going on between you two?"

"I'll tell you all about it later this week. Right now, I need to get through this day."

Barb squeezed my hand, but I still wondered if I would make it without collapsing.

Chapter Ten

Whe n I crawled out of bed on Monday, my head ached. I took an aspirin and looked at the clock. The law office of George Briggs should be open now. With luck, he'd agree to see me today or tomorrow. I called and found he had an opening at 10:00 that morning. Perfect.

The temperature had turned so warm I needed only a sweater. I could imagine shoppers rushing through the malls in their shirtsleeves as they tried to finish filling their Christmas lists.

Parking near the courthouse always presented a challenge, but that morning I got lucky and found a place on the street only two doors down from the offices of Briggs and Holt, Attorneys at Law. I'd arrived early with the hope of talking to the office staff about Nancy before my appointment with her boss.

A young woman dressed so conservatively she could have passed as a nun except for the tiny bar jutting from her pierced right eyebrow greeted me and offered me coffee, which I gladly accepted.

"You worked rather closely with Nancy, I suppose," I said, pulling the chair she'd offered me closer to her desk.

She rolled her eyes so high she ran the risk of popping the bar out of its piercing and into the ceiling. "Most of the time she worked on her own. She had her own office down the hall, right next to Mr. Briggs's and across from

Mr. Holt's. The other staff had to put up with her more than I did. Betty won't come back from her foot operation until after Christmas, and Liz called in sick this morning. The other paralegal, Donna, went over to the courthouse to file papers on a case. Papers Nancy worked on, I think."

"That's too bad," I said, "I'd hoped to talk to all the people who worked with Nancy."

"But you have an appointment with Mr. Briggs."

"Yes, I have an unrelated legal matter to discuss with him. But it could have waited. Talking with you and the others was my real purpose this morning."

"She belonged to your church." Her hesitancy hung in the air like strong perfume.

"For many years before I came there."

"Did you like her?" She stared at me, measuring my response.

"Not very much," I admitted. "I'd like to find some information to assist her husband. I don't think he killed her."

She released her breath with a whoosh. "Even if I probably don't know anything to help poor Mr. Huff, I'll gladly tell you what I do know. But I can't talk openly here. Can you meet me for lunch?"

"Name the place."

"Not anywhere near the courthouse. Too much chance of running into someone from the office, like Briggsy— oops, I mean Mr. Briggs."

Excitement tickled my nerve endings. If she didn't want anyone to know she had talked to me, she might plan to tell me things someone would think she shouldn't.

"How about a fast food joint? My treat," I said.

"Super. The people from this office would rather eat elephant droppings than go to a fast food place. Do you know the Wendy's out near the mall on Route 40?"

I winked at her. "Like my own kitchen. Except Wendy's doesn't throw away as much food because of bad preparation."

She laughed. "Lunch with you is going to be fun. Meet me there at 11:30. That way we'll beat the crowd."

"I don't even know your name."

"Jennifer Glover, but call me Jen. Oh, here comes the boss man now."

I turned and faced George Briggs just as he came into the outer office from the hall. He smiled at me but gave Jen a slightly disapproving look. "You didn't buzz me to tell me Pastor Shaw was waiting."

"Oh, I only got here a minute or two ago," I said. The young woman gave me a look full of gratitude.

He motioned toward the cup in my hand. "Long enough to get coffee, though. Has Jennifer kept you entertained?"

"You bet. We talked about our favorite restaurants."

"Don't listen to her recommendations," he teased. "The only places she frequents either get closed twice a year by the board of health, ask if you want fries with that, or think macaroni and cheese qualifies as a vegetable."

Jen performed another of her eye rolls that threatened to turn the jewelry in her eyebrow into a missile. "Well, if a certain person doubled my salary, I could take all my meals at Dutch's Daughter and Frederick's other more exclusive restaurants." She propped her hands on her hips and challenged him with her stare.

Briggs laughed, pursed his lips, and gave a wise nod. "True, but then you'd gain weight like crazy and hire some other lawyer to sue me for ruining your health."

Jen threw up her hands in surrender. She picked up her phone and pushed a button. "Pastor Shaw is here to see you, Mr. Briggs. Are you available to talk to her?"

Going along with her joke, he pressed an invisible phone to his ear. "Indeed. Send her right in." Then he motioned for me to follow him to his office.

Briggs's workspace blew me away. I had expected either sterile corporate décor, featuring huge glass-covered tables for desks and a showy computer station flanked with elegant built-in cabinets to house his law books, or a cramped cubbyhole with stacks of folders weighed down by open law tomes taking up every surface.

Instead, I saw a living room straight out of a glossy decorating magazine. A small desk with a laptop on one corner and a few open files sat between two windows framed in brocade drapes that matched the upholstery of the two love-seats and three armchairs. The cool greens and creams gave the place a tranquil atmosphere contrasting with my image of the law as an adversarial profession.

"Have a seat," he urged me. The furniture felt as good as it looked. I wondered if Nancy had any part in picking it but couldn't think of a way to ask.

"My notes say you wanted to talk about the laws relating to slander and wrongful dismissal. But I'd guess you'd like to talk about Nancy Huff first."

Glancing around the beautiful room again, I imagined an old-fashioned cash register wildly ringing as its number display spun too fast for me to read the figures. "Well, uh . . ."

Briggs chuckled. "I can read minds, you know. I won't bill you for any of our discussion this morning. If you decide down the line that you need some legal help with your work situation, we'll talk again. And then I will bill you for every minute of my time. Fair enough?"

"More than fair. I'll be direct, Mr. Briggs. I don't think John Huff killed his wife."

"You hope I'll name some nefarious character who had reason to do her in. Perhaps even someone who had threatened her. Right?" His eyes twinkled with mischief. I could see why Nancy had liked this employer.

"If someone like that existed, I imagine the police would already have his name. But you still may know something they haven't looked at, haven't taken into consideration."

He walked to the window, pulled back one of the beautiful drapes, and looked down on the traffic passing on the street below. "Nancy stayed on top of things. She handled them before they grew out of proportion. That quality made her invaluable in this office. People will tell you she could make life hard for others she lived with or worked with. No doubt you've experienced that for yourself. She made people mad, but never angry enough to murder her."

"Did she have a feud going with anyone in the office?"

"The secretaries stayed out of her way. Donna, the other paralegal, and she snapped at each other from time to time, but Donna's the kind of person who gets too lost in her work to care very much what people say or do. She couldn't carry a grudge if you gave it to her in a metal box and threw in a wheelbarrow to haul it around."

I sighed at the dead end Nancy's work appeared to offer my hunt for evidence. "So the bottom line is that they got along."

"Nancy did good work. Donna doesn't really take anything else into consideration. I can also tell you we sat down for a staff meeting last week to discuss the topic 'Where were you when Nancy died?' "

I felt my jaw hanging open. "You thought someone here might have had something to do with her death?"

He gave me a look that made me feel as if I had told him I not only believed in Santa but dated him on alternate Fridays. "We needed to talk about our feelings over losing Nancy. Her death left a hole in our staff, and we'll have to adjust to a new person in her spot. She may not have been popular, but she was dependable."

"Of course. I'm grasping at straws. It hurts to see John in jail for a murder he didn't commit—in my opinion—and even more to think of him going to prison for it."

He broke into a broad smile. "You haven't heard."

"Heard what?"

"A judge granted him bail this morning. By now, he's probably at home."

I wanted to jump on the oak coffee table, scatter confetti around the room, and cheer at the top of my voice. At last, something positive had happened since I'd promised to help John. At the same time, I knew John's temporary freedom didn't reduce his chances of conviction on the murder charge.

"Could we talk a little about my personal situation?" I asked.

We spent the next twenty minutes going over my concerns about Alvin's threats to have me dismissed.

"I'd guess this man won't get far with his attempt to get rid of you," Briggs said. "If he does, you'd have a strong case in court. I can't give you the same assurance on the slander that you're incompetent. Proof of the kind you've listed evaporates like water from a birdbath in August. You can prove libel easier, because you can show it to the court in black and white. Pinning people down to what they've said—well, let's say they can wiggle out of practically anything in the absence of five hundred witnesses or a digital recording."

I stood and tried to stretch discreetly. "Thanks for your time and your advice."

He walked me to the door. "I have one more recommendation."

"Yes?" I suspected I knew what I'd hear next.

"Drop your amateur investigation into Nancy's death. If you haven't uncovered something by now, you'll give that bloodthirsty board president a chance to aim for your jugular without helping Mr. Huff. If the prosecutor doesn't have the evidence, a jury won't convict and he'll go free. But you could end up in court yourself. It's not worth it."

When I entered Wendy's, I saw Jen waving a yellow and red napkin to get my attention. "I already got my lunch so I could save us seats. They have a special chicken sandwich right now that's great."

Somehow I managed to keep a straight face when the young woman who took my order asked me if I wanted fries with that. I plowed through the crowd of lunchtime customers and melted into my seat.

"Hard conversation with Briggsy?" Jen asked.

"Not really. A little discouraging. He wants me to stop looking for evidence in the Huff murder."

"Wow! You're like a private eye, too?"

"Not at all. I just talk to a lot of people in the course of my work. I visit sick people and shut-ins and the elderly. People who've recently lost a loved one."

"I guess even Godzilla's family would miss him, huh?" Jen pulled a pickle out of her bun and looked at it as if she held a caterpillar. "I told them no pickle, no onion. You think they'd get something that simple right."

"Mr. Briggs painted a picture of appreciation for Nancy in your office. He said the rest of you respected her even if you wouldn't claim her as a buddy."

"Briggsy's a great lawyer and an even better boss, but he has some of that wrong. Not about how he and Mr. Holt felt about her. I'll give her points for efficiency, but I have to take them off for attitude. She treated Betty and me as mean as she could get away with. Not Betty so much, I guess. She told me more times than my sister has body piercings that my greatest accomplishment in life was making her daughter-in-law look like she had brains."

"What about the other paralegal?"

Another offending piece of pickle disappeared under the paper tray liner. "Donna? She told Nancy off about three times a year. Mostly she gets lost in her own little world, so she was happy as long as Nancy stayed out of her face. They usually worked on different things. Not friendly, you know. More like coexisting."

I decided to take a chance of spinning Jen off on a tangent. "How close a relationship to Mr. Briggs did she have?"

"Oh, nothing but work. Briggsy has better taste than that. He's also very married, if you know what I mean."

"He mentioned a staff meeting last week where all of you discussed Nancy's death."

She rubbed her eyebrow bar. "Yeah, it was the funniest thing. All of us were in church or out for breakfast when she bought the farm. Good thing. I didn't have to worry about an alibi."

"An alibi?"

"Pastor, you're going to think I'm the worst person in the universe. When I heard someone erased Nancy Huff, I had to pretend I felt bad. I had to bite my lips to keep from saying something stupid, even at the staff meeting. I know I'm not supposed to think it, but the world is a better place with her gone. I don't think Mr. Huff did it, but whoever did only did what I wanted to do myself. But I'm way too chicken."

Well, this young lady had motive but no opportunity. At least my list of suspects hadn't grown by leaps and bounds.

"I told you I'd treat," I said. "Let me pay for your meal."

"Hey, this is Wendy's, not the Ritz. I feel better for getting my feelings about the Wicked Witch of the Courthouse out in the air."

I grabbed my bag and my sweater. "Have a nice Christmas."

"Don't go yet," Jen pleaded. "I haven't told you my best Nancy story. It happened the week before she got killed, too."

My synapses buzzing, I quickly sat down. "What did she do?"

"She almost had me fired. See, we're working on converting all the records since back about the Revolutionary War to digital. It takes forever, and Briggsy put her in charge. As usual, nothing I did pleased her. No matter how carefully I typed those things, she always said I'd done it wrong. Said she had to come in early and stay evenings to correct my mistakes and get more of it done herself."

"I can imagine Nancy saying and doing that."

"Well, one morning I beat her to the office. I took the CDs she'd finished and put them with the others. When she came in, she couldn't find them. She actually hit me with her stapler. My shoulder stung till morning break. She told me they didn't belong to the firm, they belonged to her personally, and I had nearly ruined her life."

"Ruined her life?"

"Luckily for me, the ones she owned had different colored lettering than the office CDs. I pulled them out of the pile and gave them back to her, but she still didn't speak to me for a day and a half."

"What had she put on them that made them indispensable?"

"You don't think she'd tell me, do you? I tried to sneak one into the computer when she went to lunch, but I couldn't find them. She must have done a good job hiding them, because I skipped lunch, turned that office upside down, and still couldn't locate even one of the stupid things."

"Have you looked again since her death?"

"Yeah, Betty even helped me. Nancy must have taken them home. Not even a blank one. I suppose she didn't want us to touch her sacred personal records."

Chapter Eleven

On the way home, I thought about the CDs with Nancy's personal records. If Jen hadn't found the computer records in the law office, could someone find them at home? Or had someone already found them?

I stopped at the mall and attempted once more to finish my Christmas shopping—with the same degree of success as my ruminations on Nancy's CDs. In the bookstore I saw a lovely volume on the things mothers do that drive their grown children crazy. I restrained myself from purchasing it for my mother. Standing there holding it, I realized how desperate I'd become to solve my gift problems. Unfortunately that didn't rank high on my list of desperations.

As soon as I entered my house, I noticed the answering machine blinking at me. Hoping neither Alvin nor bad news awaited, I pushed the button.

"Hi, Pastor Abby." Even though she hadn't identified herself, I couldn't mistake the voice of the church secretary, Joan Kress. It sounded a little like someone shaking a bucket of gravel. "I know you take Mondays off, but something strange came in the mail today. I intend to type, copy, and fold the pageant program today if I have to stay here until midnight, so stop by if you get this."

After I opened and began sipping a diet soda, I debated for a few minutes whether I should pretend I hadn't played that message in time to reply. But Joan had a strong commitment to not bothering me on my day off. She never called me unless the matter wouldn't keep till the next time I came to the office. Honesty and curiosity won out. I punched in the church's number.

Joan answered at once. "St. Luke's, Joan Kress speaking. I haven't finished copying the Christmas pageant program, so please make this snappy."

I laughed. "How did you know you were speaking to me? We didn't get caller ID for the church office, did we?"

"Oh, Pastor Abby, excuse my rudeness. My sister has called me twice this afternoon about our family Christmas party, and I simply knew this would be her again."

"You mentioned something unusual had come in the mail. Do I need to see it today?"

"I'd guess you'll want to. It's a package with some of Nancy's belongings."

"You can't mean Nancy Huff. She died eight days ago."

"Obviously she's not the one who sent them. I checked the postmark. Someone mailed them after she died."

"I'll come right over."

"Thought you might. Well, back to my pageant slavery."

Joan didn't look up from her folding as I rushed into the office and slung my coat at the nearest chair. "Only six million more to go and I'm done," she said. "The package is on the file cabinet."

A square cardboard box sat by itself above the file drawers. Joan had cut the tape, and I could see the contents as I picked it up. CDs. I examined the postmark. Mailed Thursday, no return address.

"Joan," I asked, "how do you know these belong to Nancy?"

This time she did glance up from her stacks of papers lined up along the credenza and the deep windowsills. "Dump the stuff out. You'll see."

I walked to my desk and turned the box upside down. Half a dozen silver circles fell out, followed by a 3×5 file card. Above her signature, the card held two sentences in Nancy's handwriting: "Please keep these for me until I stop by to collect them. If for some reason I can't, send them to the St. Luke's church office."

Aha. The missing CDs Jen Glover had looked for but hadn't found in the law office. I picked them up one by one. Three had Nancy's initials written on the labels.

"Do you need to use the computer now?" I asked.

"No, I finished everything but the blasted folding. And stapling. And stacking." She gave the program she'd just creased three vicious whacks with the stapler. "Such a waste of time. The audience will just throw them away, and we could easily announce everything. That would cover the kids' movements, too." She looked at me for support.

"Some people do keep it. Maybe even put it in a scrapbook, because it has their child's name in it."

Joan sighed. "Sure. Little Hildegarde's one chance to be a star. Guess I'll be doing these as long as I have this job." She hooted. "Even with all the extra things to do at Christmas and during Holy Week, this sure beats getting real work."

"Hey," I objected, "this place is real work for some of us!"

"That's why you get the big bucks, chief. Some of us do this for a little mad money and a good excuse to avoid the nine-to-five grind."

I threw my arms around Joan and gave her a bear hug. "Some days you keep me from going crazy."

"Same here. Then other days you push me right over the edge, boss."

"Not a difficult task, even on a good day."

"Be careful. I have a stapler in my hand."

"You don't scare me. I have six killer CDs on my desk,

awaiting my attack command." Killer CDs? Surely not sent by the killer, but they might shed some light on Nancy's murder.

"I surrender," Joan said. "Back to fighting the curse of the programs I go."

As she turned toward the credenza, I touched her arm. "I suspect I know the answer to this question, but I'm going to ask anyway because it could save me time. Did you by any chance boot up any of these CDs to see if they have anything on them?"

She looked at me as if I had just asked her if she'd roasted her collie and served him for lunch.

"I didn't think so," I said.

Using the computer to check out the discs turned out swift but confusing. All of them were blank.

"Why would Nancy send St. Luke's blank CDs?" I said. "We don't have a CD burner, and I don't have one at home either. Do you?"

"No, and I gave up trying to figure out that woman years ago."

Hoping Jen Glover would answer, I called the Briggs and Holt number. I recognized her voice even before we each identified ourselves.

"What color were the labels on the CDs Nancy had the fit over?" I said.

"White, like the ones in our office, but ours have black lettering and hers had blue. Very easy to confuse. Why, do you know what happened to them?"

I looked at the discs on the computer desk. Yep, blue print on a white background. "I may have found six of them, but only blank ones. How many did you say you helped her rescue from the office collection?"

"Ten. So four are missing."

"If these are actually the ones she had in there, yes. Of course, she may have had a bunch more at home and these are just from that supply."

"Oh, you didn't get them from her house?"

"No, someone other than Nancy forwarded them to the church, but at her request. She sent them before she died, with instructions to mail them here if she didn't pick them up."

"Weird."

"Very. Thanks for all your help."

I sat in the church and meditated for a short while. On the way home, I played with the possibilities surrounding the discs. John could have mailed them, since he hadn't gone to jail until the day after the postmark. But that made no sense. He could have given them to me directly, and they didn't provide any information to help clear him. If they had, he would surely have given them to the police or to his lawyer. Maybe they meant nothing, since they contained nothing. But the pattern bothered me—first the personal records on disc at her office she had told Jen would ruin her life if missing and then the arrival of empty CDs of apparently the same brand at the church where she'd been murdered.

The more I thought about the whole matter, the less sense anything involved in Nancy's murder made. All that conjecture gave me a headache, so as soon as I got home I lay down and closed my eyes.

I fell asleep shortly before the phone woke me. I glanced at the clock as I reached for the offending noisemaker. I'd slept for twenty minutes.

"Hi, Abby. It's Ike."

I rolled to the edge of the bed and sat up. "Wow, it's really you! What's up?" Gee, nothing like impressing him with dazzling conversation.

"Turns out I have this evening off. Would you like to take in that movie we talked about?"

"Now?" I squeaked. A quick look in the nearest mirror convinced me I could, if I rushed, make myself presentable in, oh, about three weeks.

"Could I pick you up about five P.M.? We can make the early show in Frederick and catch a sandwich afterwards. No fast food Frisbees, I promise."

Raw groundhog on moldy bread would have won my approval if taken in the company of my favorite police officer. "Sure. Sounds great. I'll look for you then." Attaway, Abby girl. Knock him dead with your stunning intellect. At least I had avoided using "duh" twice or drooling on the phone so loudly he'd think I had answered the phone in the shower.

Thank heavens St. Luke's had no meetings scheduled for the evening. Had Ike asked me to go with him on any other evening that week, I'd have had to decline.

Two cups of coffee and a cold shower later, I woke up enough to face making a decision about what to wear. My cranberry pantsuit seemed like the best choice. I wanted to dress up more than jeans. I almost changed my mind when I heard my mother's voice in my head saying, "No respectable man will think highly of you if you go out with him in jeans. He'll think you chose them to encourage him to get them off you quickly."

As my sweet parent would no doubt have pointed out, I didn't get that many chances to go out with guys, and I wanted the confidence I'd derive from feeling dressed for a date. When I saw men socially away from the church building these days, they were members of our seniors group, minimum age sixty, on an outing to dinner theater or a concert.

The mantle clock in my living room moved so slowly I checked it three times to see if it had broken before Ike arrived. His jeans and plaid shirt made me feel a little overdressed until he said, "You look really sharp in that color." The loose sleeves hid his biceps, but the freckles hadn't faded, and the smile made me melt a little inside as fast as ever.

I excused myself and hurried to the bathroom. I didn't

want a single moment of our evening interrupted by caring for nature's necessities. I walked through my home office, past the kitchen and dining room, and down the hall to the front door, where Ike stood waiting.

As I approached, his eyes widened. All expression left his face. I touched my hair in a reflexive move. It felt okay. Then he burst out laughing so hard he wrapped his arms around his ribs and fell against the wall.

"What's wrong?" I demanded.

Between outright guffaws and held breaths meant to stop his uncontrollable laughter, he managed to say, "You . . . you . . . Your tail . . ."

I reached behind me. When I pulled up my pants, I had caught the jacket to my suit in the waistband. I shrugged. Big deal. Hardly the comedy act of the century. "All fixed. I'm ready to go now," I said.

He hugged his ribs a little tighter. "No, not yet." Another burst of laughter exploded. "I apologize. I just can't help it. You . . . need to check some more."

I held out each shoe in front of me where I could see it. Nothing stuck there.

Still giggling, Ike reached out, took me by the shoulders, and gently turned me around. A white trail stretched down the hall and out of sight.

I gasped. "That's what I get for buying a better brand of toilet tissue. The generic kind would have torn off at the first corner."

"I could tell from the start that you're a person of superior tastes."

Then again, he hadn't eaten anything I'd attempted to cook yet. I pulled the tissue from the left side of my pants where I'd snapped it into captivity as I drew the pants up. "I'll wrap this back on the roll, and we'll be on our way." I could have left the paper lying on the floor, but I needed a moment to stop feeling as if I should find the nearest large rock and crawl under it. Ike needed the time to compose himself too, before I was arrested for assaulting an officer.

I rolled the telltale trail back into place. After all, it did cost more than the store brand, and a person facing the loss of her job had to guard against extra expenses. The roll of tissue now looked as if a ghost had gotten its head caught in the apparatus and ripped it off in an attempt to escape.

I tromped down the hallway, feeling like the Duchess of Dumb, the Countess of Clumsy, and the Baroness of Buffoonery rolled into one.

"Ah, my lady, your chariot awaits." Ike opened the door, made a wide arch with his right arm, and bowed at the waist.

I'd heard that a good cop could read minds, but I hoped this gesture qualified as a coincidence. He certainly didn't need to know *all* my thoughts. I inclined my head with what I hoped passed for a regal recognition of an inferior's service.

"Busy week ahead?" Ike said.

I wondered if he imagined me spending days rewinding toilet tissue back to both bathrooms in the parsonage and the various restrooms at church. "Yes. The worship and music committee has to resolve the Christmas tree issue, I can't get out of going to a party thrown by one of the parishioners, and we have a board meeting. One joy on top of another. Does your week top that?"

"Nope. Unless someone takes the entire crowd of shoppers hostage at a local mall, my week sounds like a piece of cake compared to yours."

"Oh, I forgot pageant practice. At least I don't have a part. I can sit there and veg as long as I put in an appearance."

His stomach growled. "Where would you like to eat?"

"Wherever suits you."

"I didn't get a chance to eat lunch. Any place that serves

food quickly meets my requirements. But I meant it when I said no fast-food Frisbees. And we'll see the film first."

"But if you're hungry . . ." I objected.

"A little delayed gratification is good for the soul." Even in the semi-dark of the car his smile gleamed at me. "I'll take the edge off my hunger with some buttered popcorn. If you're extra nice, I'll let you have some. Maybe even let you wipe your greasy fingers on my shirtsleeve."

My mind conjured up a picture of my hand rolling up that plaid sleeve and caressing the muscles between wrist and shoulder. A little oil on my skin would be a small price to pay for the privilege. "Gee, I suspected I'd have a use for that toilet tissue before the evening was over," I said.

We looked at one another and broke into the kind of laughter that clears the air, removing any lingering discomfort.

At the cinema we eagerly scanned the list of features. Neither of us had bothered to check the paper to see what was playing, which I took as a good sign. However, unless we wanted to wait more than half an hour, we had to choose between the fifth installment of a horror series and an inane teen comedy.

"Guess you'd rather skip the body count feature," Ike said.

I nodded. "Too much like reality. Remember, I have a board meeting this week."

"Not to mention a party so exciting you classify it as one you can't get out of."

"Charlotte's party doesn't threaten me with dismemberment, though. At least I don't think it does."

Though silly beyond belief, the comedy had some good lines that made us laugh. We ate our way through the largest tub of popcorn with extra butter, frequently bumping fingers as we grabbed for the yellow kernels. Ike had a dab of butter and a particle of popcorn caught in the right corner of his mouth. With great restraint I kept myself from leaning over and licking those remnants of our snack away. While I stared at his mouth, he looked at me in the dimness of the theater. Then he licked his lips slowly, circling them with his tongue twice.

"Did I get it?" he asked.

"Oh yeah."

Strangely for such a stupid movie, it ended all too soon. Wet snow clung to our eyelashes as we headed for the car.

"I'm still starved," Ike said. "Know someplace we can get decent food fast?"

"Do you like Chinese?"

"Sure."

I suggested a Chinese restaurant that trumpeted its buffet. "I've never actually eaten there," I warned. "It could be horrible."

"As long as we don't see an ambulance flashing its lights in the parking lot, I'm willing to give it a try."

The restaurant exceeded our expectations. Full of excellent lo mein, I leaned back in my chair. "What's next?"

I should never have asked that question. A beeper that I had somehow failed to notice hanging from Ike's belt began to chirp like a tiny cricket. He took his cell phone out of a coat pocket and pushed one number.

"It's Trooper Eichelberger. You beeped me? . . . Someone already there or on the way? . . . Good. I'm in Frederick. I'll drive home, get the patrol car, and go straight to the spot."

The server had left the check on the table. I snapped open my fortune cookie, popped it into my mouth, and chewed.

"I'm really sorry," Ike said. "I have to go to work." He gave me the funniest look. Searching to see how disappointed I felt, perhaps?

Since someone had told me it was bad form to read the fortune before finishing the cookie, I still had the strip of paper folded in my palm. I stretched it out and held it closer to the light.

"Disaster will strike when you least expect it," the slip read. *"Prepare to seek refuge."*

Chapter Twelve

Our attempts at small talk on the way back to Thurmont floundered on what I sensed was our mutual disappointment at the interrupted evening. Tension infused Ike's body. He glanced over at me several times, obviously wanting to speak, yet reluctant to do so.

"Look, you're going to find this out immediately anyway, so I might as well tell you. But you didn't hear it from me, got it?"

"You mean officially."

"Yeah."

A shiver went down my spine. John Huff. Had to be. "Has something happened to John?"

"Not exactly."

"Well, let's not play twenty questions. Exactly what has happened?"

He gave me one of those knee-melting grins, the kind that made his blue eyes gleam as if lit from inside.

"I thought theologians enjoyed wandering around in murky ideas."

"And I thought state troopers weren't allowed to torture people."

The grin again, a little wider. "That only goes for the ones we arrest. No rule against torturing the people we date."

This called for desperate measures. "Are you ticklish?" I asked.

"Huh? Ticklish?"

"I'm considering digging into your ribs with my nails until you either collapse in laughter or tell me about the page you got."

He turned the steering wheel sharply to the right, then jerked it back to the left. "Ooh, a threat against a police officer. Very serious offense."

"I'll risk it."

His voice went down an octave. "You owe me another dinner, one that ends more normally."

"Precisely the next words I was going to say to you."

"Now about Huff."

"Yes. Tell me about John, please."

"The dispatcher told me we got a 911 call for his address."

My stomach dropped between my knees. "No. Tell me he didn't commit suicide."

"Not even close. The call went to the fire department first."

"The fire department? A fire at his house?" Gosh, I must have set a one-day record for sounding like Einstein. Of course a fire.

"Yeah. Someone set off a little combustion inside the house."

"Someone. Not John?"

"No, he's clear on this one. He hadn't left work yet."

"How bad is it?"

"No idea. Look, you have to find this out from someone else before you come galloping over. Could you call somebody who's going to know about this so you have a way of explaining why you're there?"

I gave him my highly offended stance, stretched neck, raised left shoulder, and all. "You're assuming I can't exercise enough restraint to stay away."

He laughed the loudest he had since he'd seen the tissue trail marking my progress through the parsonage. Probably the darkness had made him miss my gesture indicating my taking of offense. "I'd bet on a six-year-old to stay out of her Halloween candy first."

Well, maybe he hadn't missed the gesture in the dark. Maybe he'd immediately disregarded it.

"I'll call Dora. If the news is out, she'll have heard it. If she hasn't, I'll call John's son and daughter-in-law. If that doesn't work, I'll call the firehouse in Thurmont and ask if they have any suggestions for putting a little excitement into my evening."

Ike gave an exaggerated sigh and shook his head slowly in a wide arc several times, as if doing exercises for his neck muscles. "Guess that tells me where a show and dinner with me ranks, if you have to go calling the local public safety divisions to pump up your level of excitement afterwards."

Now I had my turn at laughing. "You pulled the oldest trick in the book, I'd say. If the date turns into a horror show worse than the film we passed on, you just get a friend to call you so you can claim an emergency and get out of it quickly and without question. Nice spin, I have to admit, using a pager instead of a phone."

Ike stared at me so long I worried he'd drive off the road. Then he did exactly that, pulling off onto the shoulder and putting the car into park.

"What's wrong?" I said.

"The way this evening got chopped in two. So we'll have to fast-forward to the ending."

He reached over, grabbed me, and kissed me like a sailor heading off to a six-month tour of duty in the Arctic Ocean. Icebergs could have melted from that kiss.

He released me and put the car back into drive. "Now let's get you home before I get fired or sent out west to

Garrett County until I have all the years in I'll need for retirement."

By the time I stepped out of the car in my driveway, I'd cooled down enough to notice the shrill wind. Ike waved and pulled away in a swirl of leftover fall leaves and snow flurries.

As soon as I hung up my coat, the phone rang.

"I saw you get out of Officer Stud Muffin's car," Dora said, "and I want a full report with all the details, but you'd better get over to John Huff's first. The place is crawling with firefighters and their equipment."

I put all the innocence I could muster into my voice. "A fire at his house?"

"Why do I get the feeling I'm telling you old news? You bet it's a fire. At least I'd guess the fire company didn't hurry out there to get John's cat down from a tree. I have a raisin pie fresh out of the oven sitting here, begging me to cut it and serve it. When you get back, come on over and have a piece. Of course, you don't get a bite until you spill the beans."

"Raisin? Good. Raisin pie doesn't drive me crazy."

I heard Dora shove some objects around on the counter in front of her. "Did I say raisin? What was I thinking? This pie calling out to be eaten is a sour cherry with a crumb topping."

"You wicked woman. God will punish you." My stern tone collapsed into a giggle, spoiling my clergyperson-in-judgment effect.

"No, he won't. I have friends in high places. Oh, my, what's this sitting behind the cherry crumb? Sniff, sniff. I do believe an apple pie found its way into my oven. Now how did that happen? I was sure I only put two pies in. What am I going to do with this extra pie?"

I forbade my salivary glands to react to her bribe. "You're a hard woman, Mrs. Knaub."

"Remember that old guy on the TV ads who used to say

it took a tough man to make a tender chicken? Well, he had nothing on me." She hung up.

At least I had my source about the fire that wouldn't point to Ike, as well as sufficient motivation not to spend hours on this pastoral call. I considered zipping out the door immediately but decided jeans and a sweatshirt made a lot more sense for scoping out a fire scene.

The lights from the various emergency vehicles lit up the place like the midway of the Great Frederick Fair on the first night of its September run. I pulled my car off the road a hundred feet or so past all the action, got out, walked around the far side of the car, and promptly slipped into a ditch.

Thank heavens the temperature provided nicely frozen ground. I might get a bruise on my left thigh, but at least I wouldn't have to explain big clumps of mud on my jeans. I brushed off the few stubborn leaves that clung to the denim.

Suzie came running up. "Oh, Pastor Abby, I just told Bill how much I wished I had my cell phone with me so I could call you. Are you all right? I saw you fall."

Images of the paper trail flashed across my mind. "I'm fine. My day has gone like that. I'm trying out for the role of Abbess of Awkward."

Her eyes widened. "Wow, you're really thinking of leaving St. Luke's? Is it because of Mr. Porter?"

Marvelous. Not only did I have a witness to my clumsiness with absolutely no motivation to keep quiet about my lack of grace, I also had to deal with the obvious spread of Alvin's campaign to oust me from the parish.

"No, I have no intention of leaving. I'm planning to stay until they have to pull my cold, dead hands off the rails of the pulpit and carry me out the door on their shoulders."

Now I had added Olympic-level tactlessness to my award-winning display of klutziness over the last few hours. Eight days before, I had found her mother-in-law lying lifeless in the sacristy, and here I had made a joke out of being removed from the church as a corpse. Nice going, Abby. Pastoral sensitivity at its highest. Maybe Alvin was right about me.

Alvin, right? Sure, the day trained muskrats could perform the sacraments.

Suzie frowned and bit her lip. "Um . . . okay. Glad you're not leaving. Let's go find Bill and John and see what they've learned about the fire." She put her arm around my shoulders as if the fall had shaken me, maybe addled my brains. It hadn't. That kiss in the car by the side of the road, on the other hand . . .

Bill jumped when his wife touched his arm, then looked at me. "Pastor. Thanks for coming. How did you find out so soon?"

"From my neighbor, Dora Knaub." I wondered if that would suffice as an explanation. From his nod and the quick return of his gaze to the house and the people milling around it, I knew he'd accepted it.

"Dad's over there with the fire chief. They took him inside so he could tell them if anything was missing and give them some idea of what the fire destroyed. We don't know yet how bad it was, but the roof's still on, and only one window blew out."

"Which one?" I asked, craning my neck in a vain effort to see for myself.

He pointed. "Last one on the left. Used to be my bedroom when I was a kid, but Mom converted it years ago to a combination sewing and computer room."

"Did she do much computing at home?" I asked. "I know she used computers a lot at work."

The snow flurries had begun again in earnest, and Bill wiped them off his eyelashes. "Yeah, she did. Spent hours in that room. Dad would come in and sit there watching her until she'd tell him he made her nervous and should go back to his TV."

Ah, a fond picture of the warm Huff home. "Did she bring a lot of work home from the office to do there?"

He shrugged. "I have no idea. Why, do you think someone could have set the fire to destroy records that belonged to Briggs and Holt?"

I evaded answering that one. "The fire chief thinks the fire was set?"

"So far that's all he's told Dad. Unless they've said more since they took Dad inside. Here he comes now."

John approached me, grabbed my hands in both of his, and pressed. "Pastor, you're an angel to come out here on a cold night like this."

I squeezed back. "If I can help in any way, John, please tell me. Will you need a place to stay tonight?"

Suzie jumped in immediately. "No, he's coming over to our place straight from here. But thanks for asking, pastor."

John gave me a weak smile. "Yes, thanks for asking. I've been enough trouble already."

"How bad is the damage inside?" I asked.

"Not so terrible. The sewing room got the worst of it. Soot all over the walls, the carpet looks like the bottom of my barbecue grill, and the computer could pass for some weird piece of modern art. Something you'd see in a gallery in Washington with a title like 'Striking Back at Technology.' A lot of ash from burned papers sitting in soggy clumps across the room."

"Nancy would never have left piles of papers scattered around," I said. "Somebody must have put them there."

John nodded. "Or stacked them to start the fire, and then the hoses did the spreading. I don't know what the place looked like when the fire trucks got here, but I'm grateful the whole house didn't go up in smoke."

I gave him a hug. "You're a brave man, John Huff."

He blinked back tears. "I'm a tired old geezer who can't keep himself out of trouble. But thanks for the thought."

I saw Ike talking to a trooper in uniform and two fire fighters. "Excuse me. I think I'll ask Officer Eichelberger a few questions. Did you get any new information from the fire chief?"

"He already told me I can't get back in tomorrow," John warned. "Good luck collecting answers. I didn't get many. But I guess they can't say much until they do their investigation, especially since they've decided it's arson."

I'd had enough of visiting crime scenes for one month. The four of us joined hands, and I said a quick prayer, offering thanks that the fire had hurt no one and asking for a night of quiet rest for all of us.

Then I trotted over to the spot where Ike and the three other men stood watching the slowing activity at the front of the house. "Could I speak to you a moment, Trooper Eichelberger?"

"Who's this?" the other officer asked Ike.

"She's John Huff's minister," he answered. "She conducted Nancy Huff's funeral and knows the principals involved in that mess."

The trooper's eyebrows shot up, but he nodded, so Ike and I walked a good twenty feet closer to the road.

"What are the fire people saying about this?" I said.

"Not much yet. Whoever set the fire didn't do a very good job if he intended to burn the whole house down. Messed up the computer room real good. Definitely used an accelerant, but only in the one room. No sign of a timed or remote device, so I think we can figure John didn't arrange this on his own to help his chances on the murder charge."

"You mean the real murderer could have done this to destroy evidence that might point to him or her."

He stuck his hands in his coat pockets and shuffled his feet. "Or maybe John had someone else, possibly his son, start the fire to get the legal authorities thinking in that direction."

"Not likely," I objected. "Bill has made it known that he suspects his father's guilty. That opened a gap between them that argues against Bill colluding with his dad that way."

Ike stared silently at the collection of Huffs under the oak tree. "They seem friendly enough now. Maybe Bill decided to cut his losses and settle for losing one parent instead of two. But I admit it has me thinking we need to look again at other suspects."

He took a step toward me. "On a totally different subject, I enjoyed our date tonight. Except for the interruption, of course."

"Me, too." The wind picked up, and I shivered.

"Good to see you've cooled down," Ike said. "For a while there in the car, I thought you had more chance of a major meltdown than this house did."

I swatted him a good one on his upper left arm. "You should talk. That little side trip onto the shoulder of the road put us both at risk."

I glanced over at the men who still waited for Ike. They'd noticed the smack I'd given him and had stunned expressions on their faces.

"See what I mean?" Ike said. "You're so hot you've almost singed those poor guys' eyebrows off from eight yards away."

I froze my hand a third of the way to a repeat performance on Ike's arm. The eyebrows of the three watchers jerked but didn't crinkle or dissolve. "You really think I'm hot?"

Now where did that come from? If I couldn't very well pound him into the ground in front of another policeman, I certainly shouldn't encourage this line of discussion. Or should I?

The grin I saw absolutely did not qualify as professional

for a law officer. "You're the hottest minister I've ever seen. Besides, the heater in my car still works. I didn't need to pull that off-the-road stunt to keep from freezing."

"That, my dear trooper, indicates your heat, not mine."

He took another small step closer. "So you think I'm hot too, huh?"

Thank heaven even trained investigators can't see a major blushing attack in the dim light of a December evening. "What will those men watching us think?"

The grin got worse. "They'll think you attacked me because you're so hot for me you can't control yourself." His wicked laugh floated over the cold night air.

"Then we need to walk over there and destroy their misconceptions," I said.

"Be careful you don't confirm instead of dispel."

I considered whether another swat would be worth it, with the consequences falling where they might, but wisely (for the first time that day) restrained myself.

When we reached the three observers, I smiled at them. "Thanks for the job you've done for Mr. Huff tonight," I said. "You poor guys have fires and crimes to deal with, and then you have to work with this joker, too." I motioned toward Ike.

The other trooper gave me a smirk almost as evil as the last one I'd seen on Ike's face. "Uh, right, ma'am."

Flying ferrets! Ike had known exactly what lay in the minds of these guys. And my effort to dislodge that had cemented their ideas.

"Goodnight, gentlemen," I wished them in my most professionally detached voice. "I hope you have success with your investigations."

The officer smirked again. "Good luck with your plans, too, ma'am."

"Where's that apple pie?" I demanded. My coat had missed the kitchen chair, but I didn't care one bit that it lay on my neighbor's floor in a heap.

Dora snatched it up and hung it on a hook near her back door. "You only get to smell it until I hear all the good stuff."

I sank onto the chair I'd originally designated for my coat. "I surrender. The quicker I give in, the quicker I'll get pie."

"Glad you see it my way." Dora swung the apple pie in my direction, close enough I got a good whiff but well out of my reach in case I gave in to an impulse to grab it and run.

"You'll never believe this day," I said. Then I gave her the complete rundown, including the lunch with Jen, the toilet tissue disaster, and the happenings at the fire scene.

"Well, you're going to have a terrific rest of December."

"Why do you say that?"

"You've used up all the bad luck one human being could possibly squeeze into one month. But not all the pie." She cut me a quarter of the confection and put the plate in front of me.

"I can't eat that much," I protested.

"Apple pie? Since when? Get started and prove me right."

Good guest that I try to be, I immediately obliged her.

"So John Huff didn't kill Nancy," Dora mused. "Whoever set this fire did."

"That's what I think, and I suspect Ike does, too. But he hedges his bets with the possibility that John wants the law to think that way and got someone to help him out by setting the fire."

"The John Huff I know couldn't calculate that well. Maybe his daughter-in-law could, though."

"But why would she want to? If the police start looking for another suspect, both her husband and her father are candidates. Heck, even she is."

"So you can't tell me who did it."

"I can't even tell you what I'm having for breakfast to-morrow morning."

"Oh, I already know that," she said, shoving the rest of the pie into a paper bag. "At least try to make it last until supper."

"Spoilsport."

She pulled the bag back to the edge of the table right in front of her. "Hey, I don't give pies away to people who call me names."

"All the details I just gave you more than earned me that pie."

"Oh, yeah. I suppose so," she conceded, and the pie crossed over to my side of the table again. "So what are you going to do about Trooper Eye Candy?"

"I'm taking everything but my Christmas shopping one day at a time. Everything."

"Sounds like a twelve-step program."

"Do they have one for pie addicts?"

"If that Eichelberger keeps popping up in your life, and I pray to God that he does, you may have a more serious addiction than pie to worry about."

I laughed and grabbed the bag with the pie, but on the short trip back to my house, I considered the truth of her last statement.

Chapter Thirteen

Tuesday passed without incident. Until the worship and music debacle.

Warren started the meeting on time, a near miracle in itself, since he usually rushed in fifteen minutes or so after the appointed hour. As I'd figured, we had a number of visitors who surrounded the committee members like Vandals circling the walls of ancient Rome. Or maybe the Visigoths did that. Among those wearing barbarian scowls were the Porters, the Martins, the Bakers, and the Huffs.

Anyway, I could see sweat break out on foreheads around the table. To save on heating bills, the property committee had turned back the thermostats throughout the church, so temperature hadn't caused the perspiration. These people felt a different sort of heat. Before the evening ended, I detected a little singeing of my own eyebrows.

Warren brought up the various proposals on the kinds of tree, lights, and decorations. He allowed a speaker to comment on each proposal, but he rang a large bell from our handbell choir collection two minutes after the spokesperson began. When his ringing met with dirty looks, he pointed to the kitchen timer softly beeping on the table. "Your time is up," he said. If the person objected, he repeated that sentence until peace reigned.

"Let's take the issues one by one," Warren said. Subtle

as a dead skunk swinging from the sanctuary lamp, he then ridiculed the idea of a fake tree by comparing it to serving plastic food at the church picnic. "And where are you going to store the monstrosity? In the narthex, so the members have to vault over the boxes on their way into church?"

"Pastor Abby, do you agree with Warren?" Tom Martin, the chief advocate of an artificial tree, demanded. He looked at me with a ferocity I'd never seen in him before, and I felt the terror a guilty person must have experienced as Judge Martin pronounced sentence. Had he gone over to the Dark Side and joined Alvin in his crusade to dump me?

Celia laid her hand on her husband's wrist. "Tom," she warned. He took a deep breath, gave me a sheepish look, and shrugged.

"I don't have strong feelings about the tree—its size, its type, or its decorations," I said. "I do hope we'll have one."

Warren beamed. "Perhaps this debate calls for a solution in the spirit of King Solomon. Since we can't please everyone, the committee should recommend the church have no Christmas tree. Ergo, no lights, blinking, white, or colored, no Chrismons or golden balls or little squeegees with red and green checked bows. No storage problem, no clean-up difficulties, no expense, and no more debate. I so move. Thank you for the idea, Pastor."

The room broke into bedlam. I indulged myself for a moment by imagining Warren swinging from the sanctuary lamp in the company of the skunk. Then I stood and whistled for quiet. "Mr. Weston, I do not hear a second to your motion."

"Do I have a second?" he asked. No one spoke up.

Phyllis Huff raised her hand. "I move we do things exactly the way we did last year. And that we appoint a committee to begin replacing the old Chrismons with new ones or suitable substitutes by next Advent."

Barb Johnson seconded that motion, the committee unanimously passed it, and the meeting came to a merciful end.

Though not everyone looked pleased as they filed out, a universal rumble of relief moved through the crowd.

My phone call woke Ike the next morning. "This is your favorite clergyperson," I said in response to some grunts I took for a greeting. Or maybe a command to get lost.

"Oh, hello, Pope John Paul," he said. "Can't come by for a papal audience today. Have to work. Sorry. Just send some airline tickets to Rome for week after next, and I'll see if I can work you in."

"Jump out of that bed, buster, and get over to my office right away. I realized something this morning: You don't know some CDs from Nancy came in the church mail two days ago."

"Why didn't you tell me before?"

"We'll discuss that when you get here."

Ike's car sprayed gravel pulling into the parking lot. He hurried into the church, and I heard him run to the office.

"Tell me about those CDs." His chest rose and fell from the exertion.

I pointed to the credenza. "Right there, complete with the box they came in. The note from Nancy's there, too."

He read the card and looked at the postmark. "Mailed after her death. Why didn't you call me immediately?"

"I didn't think they had anything to do with her death. After all, someone else mailed them here, and the murderer hardly sent us material that would point toward him or her."

"I suppose you already took a look at what's on them."

I looked up with the innocence of a fawn and batted my eyelashes.

He closed his eyes and grimaced with pain. "Of course you did. Didn't you think the police might want to check for fingerprints or other evidence?"

"I'm not a trained investigator." I heard the edge in my voice.

"Lady, is that the truth." An edge had entered his speech as well. "Okay, tell me what's on them."

"Nothing."

"Nothing?"

"Absolutely nothing. That's why I forgot to tell you about them. Then it occurred to me maybe some expert at the state's disposal could find something not apparent to the casual viewer." I quickly summarized what Jen Glover had told me about the CDs in the law office.

"We know about that," he admitted. "We've checked through the debris in the Huffs' house for more CDs, but we didn't find any."

"So perhaps the arsonist made off with them."

"Maybe."

I took his hand. "I didn't withhold evidence on purpose."

He stared at me until I began to squirm. "I know you didn't," he said. "But I'm more worried you might be right about John Huff's innocence. In that case, a murderer could be watching your every move."

I shivered. "I guess so."

"Got a bag?"

I retrieved one from a drawer, and he put the box with the CDs in it. "Come here," he ordered.

We hugged one another until my ribs hurt. "I don't have any evenings off till after Christmas," he said.

"Neither do I."

"Come with me to my mom's for Christmas dinner?"

"Let me think about that," I said. "Call me in a couple of days."

He grinned and smirked at the same time. "I'll try to time it so I get you back for waking me up this morning."

"Late night?"

"Domestic disturbance. Ran on and on. A cop's favorite."

The door sprang open, and in came Joan Kress. "Aha. Law and gospel in action, together." Her raspy laugh made us jump apart. "Don't mind me. I'm just the hired help. But maybe you should see this, too, Officer."

She held out a large box I recognized. "The crèche," I said.

"The Nativity," she corrected. "But look what else is in the box."

I lifted the lid. Four white gloves, the kind the altar guild used to handle the church's brass, lay stuffed inside the separated compartments, crowding the porcelain figures in their cells. I picked up a glove and examined it, then the others in turn.

"Someone ran out of packing material?" Ike guessed.

"No," I said. "Two of the gloves have the same red initials inside each cuff. N.H. The other two have C.M."

Ike screwed up his mouth like one of those bitter beer commercials. "N.H. Doesn't mean New Hampshire, does it?"

I shook my head.

"Your Mrs. Huff was one weird lady," he said.

This time I nodded.

When I got to Charlotte's house that evening, the party had already started. Cars lined both sides of the road past the next two houses in each direction. Remembering my last experience parking on the shoulder, I walked squarely down the middle of the macadam.

The Seven Dwarfs still greeted me with holly branches and bells as I walked up the drive, and the family of Donald Duck offered their presents to me again. "Bet Uncle Scrooge's box has nothing in it," I griped to myself. At least he had the appearance of the holiday spirit, something I found increasingly hard to rouse in myself.

I rang the bell at the breezeway and listened to it summon our hostess with the refrain from "Jingle Bells."

Charlotte opened the door swathed in layers of sheer green material, speckled with small red Santas. At first I thought she had on a genie costume. Then I decided she had something more Dickensian in mind. "You're the Ghost of Christmas Present!" I said.

She blinked without comprehension, then flapped her voluminous sleeves in a hula-like motion. "I guess this outfit does have a spiritual quality."

"I had *A Christmas Carol* in mind," I explained.

"Then come right on in. I've got carols playing in every room."

Charlotte had tuned into her own vision of the holiday, and nothing would sidetrack her from that. "Where should I put my coat?" I asked.

"Oh, in any of the bedrooms. Each one has a theme. I'm encouraging all my guests to do their own tour. After you have a chance to look around up here, take the stairs from the kitchen down to the rec room. I set the buffet out down there, and we're going to tell stories of our childhood Christmases and the gifts we remember best. I have a funny one about a pink bar of soap in the shape of a pig."

"Ah," I commented with a wise nod.

I walked down the narrow hallway, looking in each room as I went. The last one drew me in like a magnet does a nail. I stood in awe. Stuffed figures about the size of four-year-olds faced one another in football formation, elves lined up against reindeer. Goalposts made of pairs of six-foot candy canes connected by a row of gumdrops stood against the walls behind the two lines of players. The elf playing center held a turkey between his hands instead of a football.

The second bedroom featured angels made from handkerchiefs, pipe cleaners, and aluminum foil. Dozens of them floated in the air, hanging by invisible threads. A fan placed in one corner kept them fluttering gently across the night sky painted with fluorescent stars on the ceiling.

The third bedroom had so many reindeer crammed into

it, every one of them made from some variety of pinecone, that I felt claustrophobic just standing in the doorway.

I skipped the fourth bedroom.

The darkened living room glowed with an eerie light. I crept in and looked around. At either corner of the longest wall stood a Christmas tree. Well, the shape of one, anyway. One glowed blue, the other sparkled red.

I touched the blue one and realized what made up the trees. Dozens, maybe hundreds, of mayonnaise jars had been stacked together in pyramid form. Space at the mouths of the jars allowed strings of tiny lights to enter and fill the containers. Not sure whether anything connected the jars, I jerked my hand back, fearful of starting a landslide of glass and wire.

My college ring struck a glass edge, and a "ping" echoed through the room. I prayed the trees wouldn't cascade and bury me.

"There you are!" Charlotte said. "We thought you'd left or gotten lost. Have you had a good look around?"

"Oh, yes. Your house is quite an experience."

My hostess beamed. "I call it my Christmas fantasia. Friends tell me I go to too much trouble, but turning the place into a holiday heaven gives meaning to my entire year."

Though holiday hodgepodge seemed closer to the truth, I smiled and glanced around the room with an expression of delight. If Charlotte could read minds, I was in deep trouble, because the pleasure came from the thought that my relatively bare house provided both a quieter and more attractive atmosphere.

"However did you collect so many jars?" I asked.

"I had a dream of creating this room exactly the way it stands. We ate BLTs with mayo and seven-layer salad all summer for three years."

People packed the Bakers' large rec room from wall to wall. A jolt hit me when I saw John Huff and Frank Teller in animated conversation, like old friends renewing an acquaintance. Suzie's and Bill's expressions and body language told me they had recently had an argument. Both of them spoke to Phyllis in turns, but neither involved the other in conversation.

Thankful that Charlotte cooked much better than she decorated, I loaded my plate with Christmas goodies and headed toward the punchbowls shaped like Victorian skaters, complete with muffs and long fur-trimmed coats.

"Watch out for the green punch," Warren whispered in my ear. "It packs a wallop like a kangaroo's kick. Our diaphanously veiled hostess has hit the green sauce rather consistently for the last hour, and she's beginning to sway, like a palm tree in a hurricane."

"Red suits my mood better anyway," I said. "Frankly, I think I should pour my first cup over your head after the trick you pulled yesterday."

He winced. "Yes, Pastor Momma, I was a bad boy. But I couldn't resist the opening you gave me, suggesting anything we did would get your approval as long as we had a tree. Immediately it popped into my mind that having no tree at all would incense everyone."

I patted him on the cheek. "Something you have a talent for."

"Glad to be of service." He surveyed the room as he drank from his punch cup, which contained the dangerous green variety. "Gee, you can tell Nancy isn't here this year."

"How?"

"No one looks insulted," he said. He wandered off toward the sandwich table.

Tom Martin offered me a desert plate. "Have a piece of red-velvet cake."

"No thanks," I responded. "I'm fighting my way through a small mountain of hors d'oeuvres and cookies."

"Some party, huh? I'd better get back to Celia. She fades fast at these things."

Celia did look pale, as if Charlotte's house had taken something out of her. She smiled and gave me a weak wave. Tom handed her the cake he'd offered me. She took two bites and set it aside. Though she appeared to lead a normal life, her MS did sap her energy. Tom's watchfulness probably both reassured and annoyed her.

"I hope you have your pastor's report ready for tomorrow's board meeting." Alvin startled me out of my reverie.

"Have I ever come to a board meeting without one?" I replied. Actually, I had it on my computer, but I hadn't entered the last few details or printed it out yet. Tomorrow morning I'd take care of that.

"I'm curious to see how many visits you've listed," my nemesis said. "I intend to ask which of them are true church visits and which you did while playing detective."

I considered emptying my plate on his ski sweater and grinding the food in until it obscured the pattern. "Only visits done for church purposes will appear on the report. Perhaps I'll add a new category this month. Time lost to harassment by the board president." I gave him a winning smile.

Alvin turned the color of the non-lethal punch and left me without another word. Would I pay for my words? Yes. Did the satisfaction outweigh my regret? Definitely.

To take my mind off Alvin, I inspected the decor of the rec room. Charlotte's husband had built several series of risers, small versions of the kind used by high school choirs. Ceramic figures by the thousands crammed the shelves. One set depicted Disney figures, like the dwarfs on the lawn, done up for holiday display.

Another array looked like something out of a Gothic horror tale or a bad dream, but somehow Charlotte had managed to convert even these to Christmas purposes. Near the dessert table, tiny bunnies cavorted in winter glee, skating, sledding, skiing, decorating Christmas trees, and marching toward a church on the steps of which stood an appropriately robed bunny minister.

"Oh, shucks," Charlotte said. "I hoped you wouldn't see that. I'm finishing a bunny church just like that one as your Christmas present."

"How nice," I responded. Even if the church had a rounded look that gave me the impression it had escaped from a cartoon, one bunny wouldn't have the overwhelming effect of this army of happy rodents. "You must have to search far and wide for so many ceramic Christmas figures."

Warren hadn't exaggerated; she was definitely swaying. "I have all the catalogs, and I do special orders like crazy. But often I buy the molds and alter them to fit what I want. It's a chore, but well worth the sweat. I cast most of my figures myself."

My assessment of her creative abilities went up two notches. Her hands looked strong enough to bend the china molds into any shape she wanted. Perhaps she could have made a go of that craft shop.

The Huff clan made their excuses to the Bakers and left. About half of the crowd followed their lead. Since I arrived late, I felt obligated to stay longer.

I found the powder room and made use of the facilities, but I had to stifle a scream when animal eyes glowed at me in the dim light. Then I realized a Rudolph toilet tissue cover was staring at me.

When I got back to the rec room, Frank Teller tapped my shoulder. "Still snooping around?"

"No, I'm too busy with my work."

One eyebrow arched. "Not the way I heard it, but it makes a good defense if people will buy it." He saluted and headed up the stairs.

Charlotte shuffled up beside me. "Thank heavens he's gone." The slight sway had become a perilous tilt to the left. "Listen up, everybody!" she shouted. "Fill your cups, because I want to make a toast."

As soon as the remaining guests had readied their cups, our hostess lifted her sleigh-shaped goblet. "I'm dedicating this year's Christmas fantasia to my old buddy, Nancy Huff, who this month made the world a nicer place by departing from it."

Chapter Fourteen

With four sermons looming on the horizon in the next two weeks, I got to the office early on Thursday. Hearing someone moving around inside, I expected to see Joan and rushed in with a smart remark ready on my lips. Instead I found Warren Weston rummaging through the sheets on my desk. The door to the credenza stood open, papers spread across the top, and the drawers to my desk and Joan's hung open.

"What's going on, Warren?" I said. My tone of voice let him know I was way past annoyance.

He turned the color of the last evening's punch—the kind I'd drunk, not the hard stuff he had favored. "Well, uh, it's sort of embarrassing."

"It's sort of a mess. I hope you have an explanation."

His stern look made me wonder if Warren could have killed Nancy. Looking for any evidence I'd uncovered would explain the disorder, since word had gotten around about my supposed detecting.

He melted into defeat. "You may as well know. I'd hoped no one would find out."

Quickly I ran through my mind whether I should stop him before he confessed something to me that as a minister I couldn't divulge, but he didn't give me a chance.

Warren's eyes teared, and he plopped onto a chair. "This is so humiliating."

I sat down across from him and waited.

"You're not going to believe me."

"Just tell me what you're searching for," I suggested.

"Well, I can't tell you that without explaining what I've done." He looked at me like a lost little boy.

"So enlighten me."

He hung his head. "You know I'm somewhat famous in the area for my marvelous improvisations during preludes and postludes."

I nodded. This didn't seem to be heading where I'd expected.

"I wanted something really marvelous for Christmas Eve. Something that would knock the socks off the listeners in the pews. Most of them think my playing too ornate. They haven't any idea what they're hearing. Many would prefer me to sound like that insipid stuff you hear on so-called Christian radio. They think Bach is some kind of imported beer."

My impatience surfaced. "Warren, where are you going with this?"

"I tried. I tried so hard. But the more I experimented, the worse it got."

"Improvising."

"Yes. I tried the familiar hymns. I tried the Renaissance stuff. I gave Bach, Britten, and Buxtehude a shot. Nothing. It got worse and worse. Repetitive. Cloying. Revolting."

What would it take for Warren to get to the point? I smoothed my hair back over my ears. "And so you . . ."

He wiped his hands from his hairline to his chin. "I copied someone else's ideas from the Internet. I found someone's transcription of a marvelous improvisation on a medley of Christmas hymns, old and modern. Glorious."

"If writers can get writer's block, it stands to reason composers can get improviser's block." I put my hand on his. "I don't think less of you as a musician or as a person because of that."

He teared up again. "But I wasn't going to admit it."

"Warren, your listeners don't worry about whether you composed what you play or whether it came from Wal-Mart. They simply know it's beautiful to hear."

"Thank you. That helps. But I'm still left with my problem."

"Ah, yes. Which is?"

"I printed the glorious improvisation and lost it."

"And you think it could be here?" If he couldn't hear the skepticism in my voice, he was using listening skills inferior to those he derided in the church members.

"I know how unlikely that is. But I'm desperate. I examined every piece of paper at home and at work. I turned the choir room upside down. I even crawled on the floor and used a yardstick to scoot things out from under the organ. Got sixty-eight cents, four breath mints, and three used tissues, but no music."

"Would you like me to help?"

"Oh, you are an angel. I've been here for hours hunting. I don't really think it's in this room, but I've run out of other possibilities. Sometimes I use the computer here to check my email when I come in to practice. I could have downloaded the transcript on this computer and printed it out. I don't think so, but I had hopes because then maybe a copy would be here."

We got to work. Warren went through the rest of the paper in the office—or seemed to. I restored order to what he had torn up.

He sighed. "No luck. Maybe I can find it again with a search engine."

I wanted to ask why he hadn't done that as soon as he discovered he couldn't locate the piece, but he had already headed out the door.

"See you Sunday," he called.

I looked over at the computer. The monitor screen was

dark, but the green light told me the system was on. Had Joan or I left it running?

It occurred to me that Warren had minored in theater in college. Had I just witnessed a stunningly effective performance?

That evening I sat in the office again, marking time with minor work items until the board meeting. Barb Johnson stuck her head around the door.

"You busy?" she asked.

"Nothing you can't interrupt. Come on in."

She looked over her shoulder as if she suspected someone was following her, then slipped in and shut the door behind her.

"Alvin has plans to sandbag you at this meeting."

"Tell me something new," I said.

"No, I mean really sandbag you. Pink slip. Out the door. Ride you out of town on a rail. He's serious. He wants your scalp." She pantomimed the last part.

"I admit I saw this coming. Thanks for the warning." I got up from my desk, walked over to the file cabinet, and removed the congregation's constitution and the official papers that made me the pastor of St. Luke's.

Barb gave me a hug. "Now that I've delivered the bad news, I'll tell you the good news."

I hugged her back. "You've reserved a nice place in a homeless shelter for me so I'll have someplace to go when Alvin tosses me out of the parsonage."

She gave me a mock slap. "You silly thing. I wanted to tell you I've checked with several of the board members and some other prominent individuals. He doesn't have the backing he thinks he does. The vast majority of the people of St. Luke's like you, think you're a good minister, and would hate to lose you."

I blinked back the tears. "Thank you, Barb. That helps a lot. I know this won't be an easy evening."

At a knock on the door I glanced at the clock. Time for the trial by fire.

"Thanks for the report, Pastor." Alvin shot his greasiest smirk at me. "Now we have some personnel matters to discuss, so I will ask you to leave the room."

"No, Mr. Porter, I will not." I glared at him, daring him to insist.

Since he considered me a lightweight, Alvin never hesitated. "You don't understand. As the president of this board, I insist you leave and wait in your office." He fluttered his tie, which showed a repeated pattern of a sadistic-looking Santa riding a reindeer bareback, crop in hand. "Someone will come get you when we've finished." With *you*, his face telegraphed.

"As pastor of this congregation, I must refuse." I took the constitution and the papers that made my appointment to St. Luke's official from my briefcase and slapped them on the table. "Apparently you failed to consider the legal documents that direct the relationship between this church and its pastor."

"I'm the head of this church, and I say you leave now." Alvin's face had turned purple.

"I disagree." Then I read the applicable sections of the documents before me.

"Sounds like you're wrong, Alvin," Barb said.

"Of course you'd back her against me," Alvin sneered. "Okay, let's examine the section of the pastoral report where she claims she visited members. I've had numerous complaints that we've lost a preacher and gained an amateur detective. One who doesn't think twice about violating people's privacy."

I took my work log from my case and held it out, open to the current month. "Though I can't discuss a few entries because of confidentiality, I'll gladly tell you what I can about most of these visits—what we discussed, how long I stayed, if I gave the person communion."

I held out my log for Alvin's inspection. When he waved it away, I passed it to the person on my right and motioned for it to continue around the table.

"So you did your job. Or say you did. That's not the problem. What about the other people who got surprise visits from you? You took on John Huff as your private cause. Instead of putting St. Luke's first, you spent your time and energy on a fruitless search for proof to clear him."

I thought of pointing out Alvin had made whether I had done my work his central issue prior to tonight, but I decided to let that go and aim for the heart of his attack. "As a matter of fact, evidence had been uncovered that points to John's innocence. So efforts to find the real murderer weren't fruitless. And if you add up the entries from my work diary, you'll see the few inquiries I made happened on my own time. I still devoted many hours to my work as your pastor."

Alvin shuffled the papers in front of him, opened and closed three pocket files, and generally stalled for time. "I suspect you counted visits as church work when you really spent those hours playing Scotland Yard. Besides, I have notes here from people who complained to me about the violation of their privacy by our minister. What do you say to that?"

"Read them," I said.

"That would be a violation of their privacy right up there with what you did." Alvin crushed his tie in his hand.

"Read only the relevant parts," I suggested.

He sorted papers again. "I can't."

"If you have a formal motion to make, then do it. If not, let's get on with this meeting. Let me remind you that you cannot dismiss me unilaterally. Only the bishop can do that."

"Let's discuss the issue of discrimination." His eyes narrowed and his nostrils flared. The mounted Santas swayed as if attacking downhill.

"Discrimination?" I said.

"You only visit the people you like." He pounded a fist on the table. "Others don't get the time of day from you. Poor old Mrs. Miller, the oldest member of our congregation, hasn't seen you in months."

"I visit her nursing home at least twice a month, including this one," I responded. "Each time I'm there, I stop and see her, and we chat. But Mrs. Miller has Alzheimer's. She doesn't recognize me and doesn't think the pastor's visited because she's expecting the minister who left St. Luke's fifteen years ago."

Alvin's eyes threatened to pop out of his head.

I knew I had him on the run. "What documents do you have that detail other incidents of my supposed preferential treatment?"

Alvin shrank into his chair.

"You have none?" I asked.

"None I can prove," he said with resentment.

"In other words, this accusation has its basis in rumor," Tom Martin said. I hadn't expected help from that quarter, and I gave him a grateful smile.

"Let's call it incomplete information," Alvin said.

"Then I suppose you do not have a motion to put before the board, and we can proceed to other items on the agenda," I said.

"This isn't over. I plan to talk to the bishop," Alvin mumbled.

"That is your right," I said. "Does the education committee have a report?"

After declaring adjournment, Alvin stormed out of the meeting without looking at anyone. I walked down the hall to get my coat from the office. When a hand reached out and touched my shoulder, I nearly jumped into the next month.

"Sorry." Suzie stepped out of the shadows. "Didn't mean to scare you. I've waited here, hoping to see you."

"Do you need to talk?"

She grimaced. "More like I need to explain. I haven't been straight with you about some things, and it's bothering me."

Oh, great. My second confession of the day. I hoped this one wasn't based on embarrassment.

"Let's go to the office," I suggested.

"I'd rather not. This won't take long. Look, Bill and I discussed what happened to his mother. I knew about Nancy and my dad, though he swears their relationship was totally innocent."

"And you believe him."

"In a way. Nothing my mother-in-law ever touched was completely innocent. I have my own suspicions of where their cozy little friendship would have ended up if someone hadn't killed her."

She walked toward the entrance to the parking lot. "Let's talk here. If anyone's still in the church from the board meeting, we can see them coming and change the subject. If we go to your office, they can walk in on us."

"All right. But I don't understand what you're trying to tell me."

"Bill worried from the beginning that his father had murdered his mother. I worried my father had. We also worried people would suspect each of us. Nancy and I didn't get along. Still, I've tried really hard to keep suspicion away from me and my family, and I've probably made things worse."

"Suzie, I don't know what the police think now. I have no reason to think they suspect any of you." I didn't add that her father definitely had a place on my own list of suspects.

"I sent them."

I stared at her in total incomprehension.

"The discs," she said with impatience. "I mailed the discs to the church."

"The ones from Nancy?"

"You got others?" she asked.

"No. I'm just surprised."

"That I bothered to mail them or that she sent them to me?"

"Frankly, I wouldn't have picked you as the logical person for her to trust with that task," I admitted.

She bristled. "I'm a responsible person."

"I didn't mean you aren't. Why you instead of Bill?"

"Who knows? Probably to annoy me. That was her favorite hobby, except for treating John like dirt and making eyes at other men behind his back. I figured she sent it to our house to make it easy to get them back. I never looked at them. Did they have anything on them?"

Why did she assume I had looked? "I gave them to the state police."

"You think they're connected to her death?"

"The wording on the card seemed strange, as if she thought she might not be able to send them herself." I caught myself before revealing my suspicion that she might have placed herself deliberately at risk. After all, why would she do that? I had no answer.

"My guess is she was blackmailing somebody," Suzie whispered.

"Where did you get that idea?"

She raised her arms and flapped them against her sides. "Probably from my imagination. Because I disliked her and expected the worst from her. Because it would justify some of the bad thoughts I had against her. Because she practiced her nastiness on me, so it's easy for me to see her torturing other people."

"She wouldn't have blackmailed your dad."

"You mean because they were friends. That's not it. He doesn't have enough money. Money fascinated Nancy. She had contempt for John because he never cared about becoming rich. Besides, what did she have to blackmail Dad with? He wouldn't have cared if people knew about their meetings. He saw nothing wrong or risky about them. After all, John wouldn't beat his head in or anything."

She blushed, realizing that had happened to Nancy.

"Thanks for telling me about the discs," I said. "I did wonder where they came from."

"You can tell the cops whatever you want. I couldn't tell you things before that might put my dad in the line of fire, but I'm confident he didn't kill the old bag. I know John, Bill, and I didn't, either. Who would have thought she'd be more trouble dead than alive?"

"Somehow this will get solved," I said.

"But you're out of it?"

"I never really was in it."

"Whatever. See you at the Christmas Eve service." She pushed open the door and walked out into the frosty night.

I walked to the office and opened the door. The darkness surprised me, since I thought I'd left a light on. I flicked the switch and gasped. Paper lay strewn from one wall to another.

"Whoever tossed this place didn't mind you knowing he did it," Ike said. He had come over as a favor, since another trooper had come out from Frederick.

"Will I mess anything up if I straighten some things?" I asked.

"No. Horn says he can't find any evidence of a breaking and entering. You've said nothing of value seems to be missing. No money, no equipment. Doesn't seem like vandalism, though. More like someone searching for something in a big hurry."

"I've had two little confessional incidents today. I'm trying to get my brain to work clearly enough I can decide whether I'll violate confidentiality by telling you what they told me."

"Hey, I know. Dora Knaub confessed she hit Nancy with a rolling pin because the late Mrs. Huff insulted her apple pie."

"No one confessed to killing Nancy. Their sins were much more minor."

"Sit down. Drink your coffee." He waited while I sipped.

"Okay. Suzie said I could tell you what I wanted to."

He opened his notebook. "Suzie Huff?"

"Right." I told him everything Suzie had said. "What do you think of her suggestion of blackmail?"

He bit the pen. "Makes some sense. Fits with the note in the box. By the way, you're getting the CDs back. Our experts say they had never been used. I thought maybe they'd had information someone erased before passing them on to St. Luke's, but Suzie's in the clear on that."

"What do you think of Frank Teller as a blackmail object?"

"Have to agree with Suzie on that, too. Who made the other confession?"

"Warren Weston, the organist. I caught him going through the drawers, files, everything in the office. Even the computer. But he was hunting for something he'd lost, possibly here at church. I can't tell you the rest, but it had nothing to do with Nancy."

"He didn't like her."

"No, they had a cat-and-dog relationship. But he didn't benefit in any way from her death."

Ike closed one eye. "One less irritation."

"Warren thrives on irritation. He probably misses her as a sparring partner."

"But it's possible he came back tonight. Or that he wasn't telling you the truth about his search earlier in the day."

"He minored in acting. He has a very dramatic personality."

He wrapped an arm around me and pulled me to him. I put my coffee down and melted into his side. "Suzie could have kept me out of the way so someone else could search the office. Maybe she was a lookout. She wouldn't come back here to talk. Warren could have returned to look for whatever he really wanted to find the first time. Neither one feels right."

"The perpetrator could have tossed the place during your board meeting. All we know is that it happened after the board meeting started and before Suzie left."

"True."

"From what you told me about that meeting, I wonder if the office mess has anything to do with Nancy Huff at all."

I shivered, and not from the cold. "Alvin couldn't have done it. But someone who wants to help him get me dismissed could have."

"I'll take you home. You're exhausted. You get a good night's sleep, and we'll talk again tomorrow morning."

"Thanks, but I need to drive myself home. Otherwise I won't have a car to get here in the morning."

"I'll come get you."

"No. You told me you work tomorrow morning. I can do this."

We walked to the parking lot. Ike hugged me hard and gave me a gentle kiss. For the first time in days, I felt safe.

Chapter Fifteen

The light streaming through the edges of the blinds told me I'd slept later than I'd planned. My head throbbed. I pulled on sweats, dragged myself into the kitchen, and ate a leisurely breakfast. Something from my conversation with Suzie jabbed at the back of my brain. Or maybe that was the stress of the last two weeks.

Dora answered my call on the second ring. "How did the board meeting go?"

"First tell me how you knew this call came from me. You don't have caller ID."

"I can see you standing in your kitchen with the phone to your ear. Now tell me about Alvin's latest assault."

"Assault is right. He tried to toss me out of the meeting so he could get the board to fire me. I quoted the constitution and official papers against that. First he insisted I had neglected my duties, but my records proved I hadn't. Then he accused me of showing favoritism in my visiting. Shot him down on that, too."

"They don't make many like Alvin, thank God."

"Hey, I had a little talk with Suzie Huff last night that got me thinking. She made a remark about Nancy making eyes at men. Know anything about that?"

A clink of a spoon against a cup marked her thinking time. "You know she worked for Tom Martin for years."

"And they were an item?"

"Oh, no. Nancy served as a kind of office wife—worshipped the ground he walked on, took care of his every need. She and Celia had words about it. My cousin who works at the courthouse overheard them. Celia being Celia, she handled the confrontation tastefully. But she made her message clear. Keep your paws off my man." The spoon clanked again.

"Anyone else?"

"I don't know anything about her current employer. You've met him. Think he had a thing for her or the other way around?"

"Not as far as I could tell, and I had a good source of information from inside the office. I guess Suzie exaggerated. Elephant tusks and egg whistles."

Dora put down her mug with a thud. "What? Egg whistles?"

"I hate to swear, but I sure feel like it at the moment. Another blind alley."

"Aha. You're still hunting for Nancy's killer."

"I'm not hunting for a thing except a good opening for my Christmas Eve homily. But all these inconsistencies keep going through my mind." I walked down the hall to the office to turn on my computer. "Nancy sending the CDs to the church. Through Suzie, of all people. The gloves stuffed in the crèche."

"Definitely things in the wrong places," Dora said.

I stepped into my study. "Oh my gosh!"

"What's the matter?"

"Somebody broke into my house. My study is a mess. Papers all over. The church office got torn up yesterday during or right after the board meeting."

"Call Ike."

"You bet."

Ike rested his hand on my shoulder. "Once again, no sign of a break-in. Anything missing?"

"No, but look at the message I found on my computer."

Ike leaned over the desk and read. "Get your nose out of other people's business, or your house will feel the flames, too."

"Cheery little note. You won't impound my computer, will you? I need it to get my sermons done."

"Naw. I'll print out the message, but this isn't worth squat as evidence. Any good lawyer would say you probably typed it yourself to get sympathy because you're under Porter's scrutiny. Who has keys to your house?"

"I don't know. Since it belongs to the church, everyone on the property committee and anyone with sufficient reason to convince Alvin to supply a key."

He shook his head. "Almost as bad as the office at church."

"Not quite. Half the free world has the key to our church, and half of them have office keys. Nobody wants to run over there to let someone in to make a copy or get Sunday School material late at night."

"When did this happen?"

I turned the computer off with a shaky hand. "After I left the house for last night's meeting and before I got out of bed this morning. I didn't come in here when I got home, so I don't know whether the invader had already visited or not. That feels so creepy, thinking someone could have done this while I was asleep down the hall."

"I want you to get some bolts for the doors. I could come over this evening and put them on. Better yet, call a locksmith and have deadbolts put on every door."

"I don't think I can do that. I'm not supposed to make alterations to the house without prior approval. Besides, I could put bolts on myself."

Ike held my chin in his hand and tilted it up so he could look into my eyes. "I'll call you before I leave work. If you haven't called the locksmith or bought bolts, I'll get them on my way home. Forget about permission. You can ask for forgiveness if somebody makes a stink about the bolts."

I leaned forward and planted a kiss on his nose. "I'll get the hardware."

"Might be even better if you slept over at Dora's the next few nights."

"She'd gladly have me as a guest, but I have too much work to do here."

"Coming to my mom's for Christmas dinner?" He hugged me to him.

"I haven't thought about it even once. I'll let you know."

"I'll keep asking until you say yes."

"I had a feeling you would."

The doorbell rang while I was mounting the last of my new door bolts at the kitchen entrance. Screwdriver in hand, I rushed to the front of the house. Frank Teller waited on the porch.

"What can I do for you, Mr. Teller?" I said. I yearned to demand what on earth he wanted, but politeness kept me at bay.

"You're home. I thought you'd be out spreading joy or suspicion across the countryside."

"Actually, I just got back a short time ago. I have a lot of work to finish, so perhaps you could tell me why you're here."

"I let you into my house. Don't you owe me the same courtesy?"

Instead of speaking, I swept my screwdriver in a "come on in" arc. We sat across from one another in my living room. I thought of his house, how much barer mine was, how vulnerable I felt when I looked at his hands.

"I understand you've complained about me to Mr. Porter." Immediately I could tell my shot had hit the mark.

He slid forward on the couch and pressed the knuckles of his fists together. "You want to pin Nancy's murder on me, or maybe on my daughter. Don't you think I've got a right to be angry about that?"

"Displeased is one thing, Mr. Teller. Hostile and vengeful completely another."

"Gee, I thought *you* were the avenging angel of Frederick County."

"Very funny." I crossed my arms and held on tight to my screwdriver. "Now that the authorities have pretty much cleared John of suspicion, I don't have any more interest in the case than other people who know the family."

He scooted back, stretched out his legs, and stuck his hands in his pockets. Apparently he meant to stay awhile. "Not according to what I hear. I hear you need to come up with some justification for your gallivanting around or you lose your job."

I tried to paste on my superior smile, the one Dora said made me look like a six-year-old with a bag of candy she'd shown the other kids and then announced she had no intentions of sharing. "Apparently you haven't talked to Alvin today. His attempt to dismiss me ran into something of a brick wall last night. A legal wall."

The corners of his mouth twitched, but no smile appeared. "Actually, I have talked to him. I'm not surprised you bested him. Alvin's not the sharpest tool in the shed, but he's a bulldog when he gets ahold of something. He contacted your bishop this morning and laid out the complaints about you he's collected."

I waved a hand with studied unconcern. "The bishop receives unfounded grievances all the time. With so little basis for Alvin's concern, and yours, I have nothing to fear from that quarter."

"Your confidence is impressive. Too bad it's going to do you no good." He jabbed a finger at me. "The bishop told Alvin he'd make some inquiries, took Alvin's list of names and numbers, and promised he'd come out here on Christmas Eve. Alvin wanted him sooner, but that's the first date he could make it. Sounds like he wasn't too happy about making the trip."

"Christmas Eve?" I could hear the squeak in my voice.

A satisfied smirk crossed his features. "Not so brave once you have to face someone who can actually give you the boot, are you?"

"Who appointed you to deliver this news?"

"Your board president."

"What do you have against me that you take so much pleasure in this? Because I asked a few uncomfortable questions in the hope of clearing an innocent man?"

"Nancy was my friend. She was there for me in a way no one else was. You tried to smear her name."

I struck the arm of the chair with my screwdriver. "That's unfair and untrue."

He stood and loomed over me. "You know what I think? I think you had an entirely different purpose in your little detective efforts than you'll admit. Do you really think I haven't figured out you hoped you could blame Suzie or Bill or me for Nancy's death? And I've figured out why. I'm on to you, Little Miss Innocent."

My fingers wrapped more tightly around the tool in my hand. "You think I'm trying to advertise myself?"

"No. Not at all. I figure you already know who the killer is, because you murdered Nancy."

"Me?" That darn squeak again.

"Yep. She was a thorn in your side. She knew you weren't up to the job as pastor. My guess is she had records that showed how badly you did your job. That's why you torched the computer at John's house. I see you're handy with tools." He nodded toward the one I held.

"I was in Frederick when that happened."

"Yeah, tell me another one. I heard you showed up at the scene of the fire looking as if you'd done some heavy work recently. Like dragged some gas cans around. And who found Nancy? You did. Who else even knew she'd be there that morning, getting the altar ready?"

"Anyone who bothered to look at the altar guild schedule in the church newsletter," I said.

"But who else would show up that early without people noticing? The pastor, that's who."

He stomped to the door, then turned and laughed. "Alvin's going to take care of your job. I'm going to take care of your freedom. You killed her, and you deserve to go to prison. I'm taking everything I know to the police. What do you intend to do with that screwdriver, stab me and hide my body in the cellar? You're toast, Pastor Shaw. Burnt toast."

I hugged myself while I counted to three thousand after I heard his car pull away. Then I grabbed my cell phone and coat and took off for Dora's.

"We're going to call Ike right now," Dora insisted.

"No, he's going to call about the bolts. He has my cell phone number. I'm not in danger," I said.

"That Frank Teller sounds crazy."

"A lot of crazy things have come to the surface since Nancy's death. I've looked for a pattern, but the harder I try, the more muddled my thinking gets."

My cell phone beeped.

"Do I have the pleasure of speaking to the proud owner of several new deadbolt locks on her doors?" Ike asked.

"No, but you have the honor of addressing the proprietor and installer of some lovely strong door bolts."

Dora giggled and raised her arms like a weightlifter showing off muscles.

"Someone's in the background," Ike said.

"I'm at Dora's."

"For a reason?" He sounded concerned.

"Well, maybe. And maybe just nerves." I told him about my visit from Frank.

"Wow. Alvin doesn't let go once he's obsessed with an idea, does he?" Road noises came over the connection, indicating Ike was in a moving car. "Did you call your bishop?"

"As soon as I downed a nice hot cup of comforting tea Dora made me. I didn't get him. His administrative assistant assured me the bishop will call me back, though heaven knows when. I asked some questions about this kind of accusation. Not rare, and the result isn't usually the pastor's dismissal. But I got the feeling that even if I'm exonerated, I'll have an uphill battle to overcome the scars."

"Well, we both know you didn't torch Huff's house."

"We both know I didn't kill Nancy," I insisted.

"Gee, now that I can't say." He cleared his throat to cover his laugh. "I suspect you could give that processional cross a mean swing."

"They say the best defense is a good offense. Could Frank have suggested I set the fire or killed Nancy to cover his own guilt?"

"We've checked him out thoroughly. He has a solid alibi for the night of the fire. Haven't checked out what he did last night or this morning, of course. Seems pretty silly for him to come confront you if he'd already done so via your own computer."

"Unless he really is a fruitcake," I said.

"Possible, but not likely. I'd guess he displaced his grief and his affection for his late wife onto Nancy, and now he finds it easier to feel anger toward you and blame you than deal with both losses."

"When did you turn psychologist?" I said.

"On days when law enforcement seems as much fun as sticking needles in my face, I consider the occupations I could switch to. I'd make a good therapist. If the client didn't cooperate, I'd throw a hammerlock on him until he changed his mind."

Dora brought me a refill on my tea. I gave her a grateful

smile and sipped it. "Back to Frank Teller, Dr. Pain. You don't think he's the murderer."

"I don't like him for any of it. He checks out at work and with his neighbors and associates as a solid man. A little reclusive, but not odd in the sense we'd need for what you're conjecturing."

"Oh, elephant eyelashes."

"Huh?"

"You know I don't swear."

"I could give you lessons," he offered.

"You're too busy."

"Right now, yes. For one thing, I intend to check out the whereabouts of one Mr. Teller last night. I'm also going to alert my superiors to expect his complaint and see if we can use that to get some more information from him. I might drop in on Suzie Huff, too. In the spirit of the holiday, you understand."

I groaned. "They'll think I sent you."

"So what? Then they'll know you have friends in high places."

"I thought I already did, as a function of my job."

"A little divine intervention in this whole matter wouldn't hurt. Take care. I mean that. Serious care."

Chapter Sixteen

Nancy's murder seemed to hang over the service more on the second Sunday following her death than it had the week before. The choir sang a sluggish anthem, the congregational responses sounded as if everyone in the entire nave had overdosed on sleeping pills the night before, and my preaching came across only slightly more lively than the obituary page in the *Frederick Post*.

I comforted myself with the thought that everyone had their minds on the Hanging of the Greens right after worship. But as soon as the postlude began, the majority of the congregation hurried out into the unseasonably warm day, leaving a tiny remnant to handle the decorating.

I chose pew candle holder duty, primarily because Alvin installed himself as the chief honcho of the Christmas tree decorating. So had our organist, possibly for the same reason.

"Did you ever find the missing music?" I asked Warren.

"Shush," he replied, then glanced around to determine if anyone could overhear us. "No. I couldn't locate it again on the Internet, either. I'll just have to settle for something mundane. Even that should be a step or two up from the way things went this morning."

"Look on the bright side," I said. "We have the pageant yet to come this evening."

"Oh, joy. That gives me the afternoon to get good and drunk so I can withstand the ordeal."

"You only have to lead the choir in one number."

"But I have to sit through the whole mess and pretend I'm not trying to inhibit my gag reflex."

I put the glass globe and a candle in the holder Warren had attached to the pew and handed him another pole. "The kids can be really cute saying their pieces."

"If none of them get frightened enough to throw up on stage."

"You're incorrigible." I took out another globe and dusted it.

"That and my musical talents make up my gift to the world."

Alvin sauntered up to us, managing to look both cocky and wary. "I understand you had a visit from Frank Teller."

"He stopped by two days ago to wish me the joy of the season." I pushed the globe into its frame, hoping the pressure I applied wouldn't shatter it.

"Then you know the bishop promised to investigate and then come to our service on Christmas Eve."

"That's only a week away, Alvin. You're expecting a lot in a short time," I said.

Warren shifted from one foot to the other. "If you'll excuse me, I'll go get another box of globes." He hurried from the nave, and I wondered if he'd return. I also wished he had taken me with him.

"Some things don't take long, once you get the ball rolling," Alvin commented. He patted his tie as if brushing off crumbs. I glanced at it. Then I did a double take.

"Nooses, Alvin?"

He frowned. "What are you talking about?"

"Your tie."

He peered down. "No. Can't you tell a lasso when you see one? And those are wreaths between them, if you can't figure that out."

I considered asking if they were funeral wreaths, but I

kept my thought to myself in the spirit of the season and the hope that Alvin would go away.

"I meant to ask Warren if the choir could sing something with a country sound during the Christmas season. I've heard some good songs on the radio." Alvin kept staring at his tie, perhaps wondering whether the lassos really were nooses. And if he could use one of them on me.

"Why don't you write your suggestion down and leave the note in his mailbox in the office? We're all so busy he's not likely to remember what someone says during the Hanging of the Greens."

Alvin pulled himself to his full height. "He should recall what the president of the board suggests no matter how busy he is."

Barb Johnson sailed over from the corner of the tree decoration. She rolled her eyes at me, knowing Alvin couldn't see her. She tapped him stoutly on the shoulder blade. "Hey, prez, we've got a problem with the tree. We need you over here to mediate a dispute."

Alvin brightened and took off for the tree.

"Thanks," I said. "I owe you a huge favor."

"Minimizing Alvin damage is my main goal for this little event. I figure Alvin's presence will help speed things up, though. The disputing parties will shut up once he arrives just so they can finish and get out of here, away from Alvin."

I chuckled. "You're evil. I like that. Santa will leave you something extra in your stocking this year for this."

"Sure. Probably another ten pounds on my thighs. Don't let Alvin get to you. Just think of him as our resident holiday turkey."

We giggled and got back to our tasks.

The pageant got off to an ominous start when the youth choir knocked over the Christmas tree set up in the center of the stage. That threw them into a panic, and they never managed to get in time with Warren's direction before their opening song mercifully came to an end. Warren leaned his head forward against the upright piano. He looked as if the teens had kicked him in the kidneys instead of sending the tree crashing.

While the four- and five-year-olds trooped onto the stage, I felt a tap on the back of my neck and looked up into incredible blue eyes. Ike motioned for me to join him at the back of the hall.

"I want you to know that Frank Teller has apparently disappeared. He did show up at the barracks to lodge a complaint against you, and I had alerted the others that I wanted a crack at him if he came in."

"Do you think he took off because of something you said?"

His tongue touched his upper lip and retreated. "I did remind him defamation of character is an actionable offense, not something we arrest people for, but a very big expense if you lose a lawsuit because of it. I also pointed out he hadn't brought a shred of evidence to back his accusations."

I felt myself pale. "You could get in trouble. The word has to be out that we're—what? Seeing each other?"

The freckles danced. Freckles in December. I sighed. The closest I could come to that would be glitter picked up from handling the children's Sunday School projects.

"I think people still use the word "dating," Pastor Shaw. I also talked to Suzie Huff. She acted cooperative and a bit contrite."

"At least she's not missing, too. I saw her come in with John and Bill."

"I have to go." He waved his hand up and down his uniform. "You can see I'm on duty."

"By the way, the answer is yes."

"Yes? To what?"

"Your invitation to have dinner at your mother's."

His smile made me think of a ten-year-old boy spying a new bike under the Christmas tree. "Great. I'll let you know the details."

I propped my fists on my hips. "I certainly hope to see you before Christmas. That's eight days away."

"You will," he promised. "Have to go. Enjoy the pageant."

I took the nearest empty chair. Someone had taken advantage of my absence to commandeer my previous seat near the front. I'll never understand why the same people who fight to sit as far back as possible in church will attack like Attila the Hun to get a place near the front at a program like the pageant.

A second grader stood alone on the stage. Quiet fell. I could hear the shuffling of feet and squeaking of chairs being adjusted. The Sunday School teacher serving as prompter motioned wildly for him to begin. He opened his mouth. Nothing came out. He closed it, coughed politely into his fist, and opened his mouth again. Silence. We waited. At last the pageant director whisked him off into the wings.

I began to wonder if our Christmas pageant should go the way of the rack and the guillotine.

We made it through the next several sets of performances, and I started to relax. Then the three-year-olds marched on stage. One little girl in a lovely velvet dress trimmed in what had to be handmade lace grabbed herself just before the signal to begin. "Mommy, I have to pee!" she yelled. The crowd broke into hysterical laughter. The mother, laughing harder than anyone, rescued her daughter and took her off in the direction of the bathroom.

The adult choir sang their one piece, a simple anthem with almost the country feel Alvin wanted. They had obviously recovered from the sluggishness of the morning. They walked down the aisle to the back to lead the congregational singing of the last carol. As he went by, Warren bent over and whispered to me, "Disgusting piece of trash, but it makes them happy and matches the rest of the evening. We survived, if barely."

The entire troupe of children filled the stage to receive their deserved applause. I jumped up from my seat to greet some of the people I hadn't seen recently. Then I saw him.

Standing at the back door where I couldn't miss him was George Briggs. He stared at me as if afraid I would dissolve before he could speak to me. Tension had replaced his usual relaxed manner.

"Good evening, Mr. Briggs." I shook his hand. "You look like a man on a mission."

"I need to talk with you about a little matter of some CDs."

I thought of telling him I didn't really have a recording quality voice, but our church choir might be willing to make a CD for him if he could wait until after Christmas. However, Briggs didn't seem in the mood for humor.

We sat on the front pew, directly in line with the glowing Christmas tree. I had turned on every light in the nave, ostensibly to present the beauty of our church bedecked for the season, but actually because I had no intention of being caught alone in a dark, empty church after my experience with Frank Teller. I'd also asked Barb Johnson to hang around until I was ready to leave. She gave me a funny look but didn't ask why.

Not that George Briggs struck me as scary. I merely felt more and more confused about Nancy's death and everything that had happened since. Even the police couldn't tell the players without a scorecard in this mess, and I had no idea where Briggs fit in.

"Jen Glover let something slip the other day," he said. "I hear she told you about some CDs Nancy had at our office while she worked on the conversion of our old records to digital."

"Yes, that's true."

"You never mentioned this to me." The edge in his voice made his displeasure evident.

"I didn't find out about them until after we talked. Besides, the ones you're talking about belonged to Nancy. She claimed they did, anyway. Jen agreed they didn't look the same as the ones you use. They had different labels."

"I got the impression the CDs ended up in your possession."

"Well, some CDs of Nancy's passed through my hands. The state police have them now. But I can tell you what they told me. The disks contain no information at all, and they never have. No one's ever put data on them."

He looked at me with open skepticism.

"Frankly, Mr. Briggs, I can't see why you're interested in Nancy's personal property anyway."

He sighed as if explaining the obvious to the idiots of the world was a burden too great to bear. "You're a bright woman, Pastor Shaw. Surely you can see that a law office handles a great deal of sensitive material. Things that could damage both the law practice and its clients if they fell into the wrong hands."

"But these CDs had nothing to do with your firm or its clients."

His hands tightened on the pageant program he held. "I can't know that for sure unless I see them."

I turned my body toward him. "The police told me nothing had ever been written on the CDs I gave them. If Nancy had other disks with Briggs and Holt records on them, they aren't the ones I saw. Probably they never existed. Perhaps the fire at the Huffs' home destroyed them, or the arsonist took them."

He nodded his head slowly, letting me know he had thought of that possibility.

I lifted my hands and dropped them on my thighs. "I can't help you, Mr. Briggs. If you contact the state police, they'll corroborate what I've told you. For your peace of mind, I suggest you do that."

"You're a lot better at giving advice than you are taking it, aren't you? I warned you that your involvement in the investigation of Nancy's murder could prove dangerous, and now sources tell me you might lose your position as pastor of St. Luke's."

"Sources?" I said.

"Ah, you know I can't tell you who. Privileged conversation." His laugh had a bitter edge.

"Since I don't think any discs of sensitive Briggs and Holt information ever left your office with Nancy, I don't think you have anything to worry about. But I understand your uncertainty, and I hope the holiday season will bring you some peace and contentment in spite of this concern."

He stood and buttoned his coat. "I only wish I could offer you the same assurances about worry."

Once he had gone, I sat and drank in the smell of the pine and the candles. Then I realized I had kept Barb waiting, so I headed for the office.

By the expression on her face, I knew something was wrong. "Hey, Tom, she's back," she yelled.

Tom Martin entered from the other room. "Pastor Abby, I have something uncomfortable to tell you, and Barb needs to hear it, too."

"I already have," she corrected.

"You realize I think Alvin has gone over the edge with some of his suggestions." The stiffness of his posture made me think of the guards in front of Buckingham Palace. "But the bishop called me as part of his investigation into Alvin's complaint. I think you've done a fine job, but Alvin's accusations and your involvement in legal matters outside your ken have damaged your standing as pastor."

He swallowed and looked at his feet. He didn't find this

easy. "I can no longer support you, and I agree with Alvin that you should go. I hope you'll tender your resignation by Christmas Eve to save us all the embarrassment of pursuing the matter. That's what I told the bishop."

He swiveled on his heel and dashed from the room. I stood motionless until Barb wrapped her arm around me. "Most of us don't feel that way. Remember that. Don't resign."

"This hasn't been a good day," I said. "I need to do some heavy thinking."

Should I quit? My mother would welcome me home with open arms. She'd rejoice at having me with her. Then she'd launch her offensive to convince me I had erred from the beginning and could have a wonderful life if I'd just let her arrange it.

Resign and go home to Mom? If they fired me, I'd learn to cook and work as a chef. I'd open my own business installing home security systems.

At home I couldn't rest. I decided to use the same method I used when a sermon had me stumped. I pulled out some blank sheets of plain paper and drew circles on the top one, filling in the various people connected to Nancy. I connected the circles with lines and made comments about the relationships. I stared at the sheet. Nothing new. I put it aside.

Next I listed the things Nancy had done at the end that hadn't made sense. Sending the CDs to the daughter-in-law she despised with instructions to send them to the church. Putting the gloves in the crèche.

These things convinced me she'd intended to send a message, but what? That she'd slipped off her mental moorings? That the whole thing amounted to a huge joke? Not funny, Nancy.

I lit some candles in my living room and sat in the dimness, running remembered scenes like movies in my mind. I pictured the last time I'd seen Nancy alive, finding her body, going to the sacristy with Ike, helping Charlotte, Celia, and Tom clean up after the lab crew.

Pummeled by the wind, the house creaked, and my candles flickered. I understood Nancy's message as clearly as if she stood beside me, speaking the words.

"Look for the thing that's out of whack."

Out of whack. I'd seen several things somewhat off since her death, but only one the day after she died.

I leaped from my chair, grabbed a coat and a couple of items from my toolbox, and raced to St. Luke's. First I drove all around the church to make sure I was alone. My hands trembled, the keys shook, and I took longer than usual getting into the church and then the sacristy.

The heritage cabinet resisted my efforts to open it. Then the door sprang open, and I grabbed the ciborium from the congregation's original building. Gently and carefully, fearful of damaging the treasured object and having one more black mark against me if my guess proved wrong, I pried off the bottom.

Onto the counter fell a CD with Nancy's initials on the label.

Chapter Seventeen

The wind had picked up, the temperature had dropped again, and St. Luke's felt creepier than a Transylvanian vault at midnight. I headed for the safety of home. Once I had bolted the doors to the parsonage and checked them twice, I popped the disc into my computer.

I looked at the clock. Too early to call Ike. Besides, this disc could be empty, too. I had enough problems without starring in a gender-bending remake of "The Little Boy Who Cried Wolf."

At last the disc information came up on my screen. Password protected, of course. At least it had something on it. I began with all the people and dates in Nancy's life. None of them worked.

Exhausted, I dozed all night at the computer, sprawled in my comfortable office chair. When my obsolescent computer took forever to reboot, I longed for the powerful new Dell at work and decided the first hint of dawn made a return to the church safe enough to risk. First I'd call Ike.

No answer. Okay, I'd call him from St. Luke's. I checked Dora's windows. Still dark throughout the house. I scribbled a note and stuck it in her kitchen storm door.

Snow flurries whipped across the brightening windows in the church office. The password screen appeared on the Dell. I thumped my forehead, but I remained stumped for more words to try. A state police expert could crack this faster than I could brush my hair. Something I hadn't done. First things first.

I called Ike. Still no answer. I paced the length of the room several times and debated whether to phone the barracks instead. I'd brought an officer to the church for nothing on Thursday. The other troopers would tease Ike about the flake he was dating. I sat back down at the computer.

An icon of a Madonna and Child I'd hung over the computer desk caught my attention. I emptied my mind of its confusion and concentrated on what I'd heard Nancy say. Nothing struck me I hadn't already tried. Then I thought of my talk with Suzie after the board meeting.

I typed in FRANK. Not that. Not TELLER, either.

For some reason, that conversation with Suzie resonated in my head. I tried BLACKMAIL. Nothing.

I ran to the church kitchen and retrieved a diet soda from my private stock. Back to the machine.

I hit the keys for MONEY. A whirr, a flash, and a menu full of documents popped into view.

My mind cleared. I knew who had killed Nancy Huff. In a few minutes, I'd know why, too.

I dialed Ike's number again. No luck. Where could he be? I'd just open a few of these and then call the state police barracks.

Half an hour later, I understood Nancy's plan and why she had thought she'd succeed. I picked up the phone, but it flew from my hand.

"You won't be using this," a deep voice said. The phone disappeared into his jacket pocket. "So you found it. I figured you wouldn't give up until you did, if it really existed. Not that I doubted Nancy. She wouldn't have attempted blackmail without the goods to back up her threats."

"How do you know I found anything?"

He produced the base of the ciborium from the same pocket that had swallowed my phone. "I stopped in the sacristy first. You must have been in a big hurry to get into that disk. Didn't your mother teach you to put things back where you found them? When did you locate it?"

"Enough hours ago to have called the police and told them what I have," I said. "So you knew to look for a CD."

"No, I only knew she had records. That made searching for them much harder, not knowing what form they'd take. But with all the equipment in that law office, it makes sense. Unlike your silly lie about telling the cops."

He threw the ciborium base onto the credenza. "They'd already have picked it up, even though your credibility must be waning with them, just like it is with this congregation. I tried to get you to let it go. You could have resigned, gone away, forgotten about the whole thing. Then you could have lived. Oh, no. You had to play Dolly Detective."

"What will Celia say?" I didn't think it made any difference, but I needed time. To think. To pray. To hope.

He leaned over me. I could see he had to restrain himself from grabbing me. "Celia won't say a thing. She never knew about my secret fund. Even though it was all for her."

I gestured at the document on the computer screen. "This was for her?"

"An idealist like you would never get it. Celia deserved things I couldn't give her on a judge's salary. Justice usually goes to the person who can afford the best lawyer. Why should the guy arguing in front of me profit while I get nothing? That's how it started. A little leniency here, a blind eye to some already questionable evidence there."

"You sold justice so you could lead the good life."

"What do you know about justice?" He shook my chair, and I bit my tongue. "For you, justice is something that happens on TV at the end of the hour. You've never watched the person you love best in the whole world deteriorate in front of your eyes, inch by inch. You can't imagine the size of the medical bills."

"You're right," I whispered. "I can't." My tongue hurt,

and I had to go to the bathroom. Now was not the time to mention either thing.

"Nancy Huff deserved to die." He wrung his hands as if he had her neck in them. "She was an evil woman. I trusted her to empty my personal drawer and destroy the notes. She agreed she'd never look at them, just eliminate them. After a few months, she told me she wasn't comfortable doing that and asked me to destroy them myself. I did, every Friday afternoon."

"Then she couldn't have had much proof to hurt you with," I suggested.

"Oh, you always did underestimate her." He laughed as if I'd told a good joke. "She suggested the day because of my schedule. That morning in the sacristy two weeks ago, she told me how she'd handled it. She made copies of the contents of my private desk drawer every Thursday. All because of my loyalty."

I jumped out of my seat. "Because of your *loyalty*? You broke your oath as a judge!"

Tom grabbed me by the arm and pushed me roughly back onto the chair. "You know less about loyalty than you do about justice. Nancy threw herself at me. She actually thought she could get me to leave Celia for her. I was patient. I thought I'd let her down easy. I explained that I trusted her and valued her work but never saw her as anything but my paralegal. She pretended to accept that. Even if I'd given her the money, she'd have sent a disk to the authorities."

Tears began to creep from his eyes, and I fought them back in mine. "I don't want to kill you," he said. "You're not evil like Nancy. Dumb, maybe even dumber than that fool Alvin Porter, but not a bad person. However, you've left me no choice."

A car honked as it passed the church, jolting Tom into action. "We have to be going. It's light already. Time for you to type your suicide note."

"The police are going to catch you. Your best bet is to give yourself up and plea bargain."

Another wild laugh echoed off the walls of the office. "Now she wants to be my lawyer. If I go to jail, Miss Big Thinker, the state will revoke my pension. Who'll take care of Celia then? You?" He removed a handgun from his jacket.

My mind traveled along the roads of Frederick County like a state police car racing at top speed. But I had never gotten Ike. He didn't know I was here or what I'd found. Now he might never know, all because I'd feared embarrassment if my hunch proved wrong.

"Type," Tom ordered. "Here's what you're going to write: 'I can't go on. My position as pastor means everything to me, and I'm going to lose it. I can't bear the humiliation.' Hey, I said type!"

"You try typing with a revolver in your temple," I said.

"It's not a revolver. It's a semi-automatic."

I pounded my hands on the keyboard. "As if I care! The hole in my head will be just as round, and my brains will spatter over this room just as far."

"Oh, I'm not about to put a hole in your head. Unless you force me to. Down the road a mile or two is the entrance to an old quarry. You're going to drive right over the edge. The car will probably explode. But you'll never feel it."

"You'll have to walk back here. The police will see your footprints."

He smiled. A palpable sense of evil filled the room. "Haven't heard the weather report, have you? It's going to snow all morning. The ground's frozen, and the new snow will cover any sign I've been there. I'll put the cup back in the cupboard and be on my way, in time to take Celia out to breakfast."

I wiggled, making the chair squeak. "It's a ciborium, not

a cup. Like a semi-automatic isn't a revolver. I need to go to the bathroom."

"You're not going anywhere yet, you stupid cow. Type what I told you."

I looked at the shelves to the side of the monitor. On the middle one sat the church seal, a good ten pounds or so of iron used to stamp baptismal certificates and wedding licenses with the name and symbol of St. Luke's. Sadness that I'd never stamp another official church document surged through me.

I'd never preach another sermon, check out one of Alvin's ties, eat a piece of Dora's apple pie, or melt against a muscled cop and feel his arms around me.

I grabbed a tissue and wiped my tears. Tom grunted and sighed deeply.

"Tell me again what to write," I said. I hit a few keys, and the CPU whirred.

"You've saved the disk to the hard drive!" he yelled. "Make it stop! I don't intend to torch another computer."

"I can't. I don't know how," I moaned.

He shoved me aside and began to type in rapid motion.

I picked up the church seal and struck him full-force in the face. His glasses snapped and flew off in pieces, blood gushed from his nose, and he sat down on the floor.

Another whack, this time to the temple, stretched him out cold. Though I never made it as a track star, I did have the second-best forehand on the tennis team.

I had punched in the first two digits to call the police when Ike came bursting through the office door, followed seconds later by Dora.

"What do we have here?" he asked, staring down at the bloodied face of Tom Martin.

"Nancy Huff's murderer, a little the worse for wear. His gun's over in the corner. Right now, I'm going to the bathroom."

* * *

I cried my way through the few tissues left in the rest-room. Images of my car going over a precipice into an abandoned quarry, with my unconscious and soon-to-be-dead body in it, pushed back into the front of my mind no matter how hard I shoved them away.

A siren announced a police car's arrival in the parking lot. A knock on the door startled me. I couldn't stay in the ladies' room all morning.

When I opened the door, I found Dora waiting patiently. "I found your note and called Ike. Then I called 911, which you should have done as soon as you found the disk."

"I didn't want to raise a false alarm," I said.

"No, instead you wanted to scare the bejesus out of the rest of us by putting yourself in the path of a killer."

"Excuse me, ma'am, but I need to take your statement." Just my luck. The same cop who'd come to the church Thursday evening.

When I walked back into the office, Ike was reading Tom his rights from a card. I supposed with a former judge you took extreme care to observe the protocol. Tom wore hand-cuffs, and he wouldn't look at me.

"Do you want to go into Frederick later to make your statement?" Ike asked.

"No, I'd rather get it over. Could I do it in another room?" I nodded toward Tom to indicate I didn't want to tell my story in front of him.

Another police car pulled in. Trooper Horn took Tom Martin outside and stowed him in the backseat. After the car left, the trooper returned, and I spent the next hour in a classroom telling him everything I could recall since I'd last seen him. Dora sat on one side, and Ike guarded me on the other, holding my hand while I talked.

My two sentinels escorted me to my car. "What plans do you have for the rest of the day?" Ike asked.

"I'm hungry." To my surprise, I felt as if I not only could

eat, but had to. "After I eat a cup of yogurt, I plan to sleep until the sun's gone down. Maybe until it comes back up."

Dora clapped her hand to her mouth. "Cup of yogurt? Not on your life. You're coming to my place. I'll feed you a good country breakfast, ham and eggs and toast with blackberry jam. Then I'll tuck you into bed in my guest-room with my grandmother's quilt, and you can sleep as long as you like or until the apple pies come out of the oven and have time to cool, whichever comes first."

"Sounds great. Am I invited, too?" Ike said.

Dora eyed him warily, probably trying to figure if he had the food or the bedroom in mind.

"You come over for dinner," she finally said. "I'll throw a chicken in a pot and make dumplings. Give the poor woman some time to breathe, Eichelberger!"

"No, thanks. I was joking. But I'll take a rain check." He looked at me, and those blue eyes and dancing freckles made me want to grab him and hold on until the last residue of shakiness inside me dissolved. "I drew night duty for the rest of the week. That's why you couldn't reach me. When you should have called the barracks right away."

"Let's not go there," I said. "I'm too exhausted to tolerate any upbraiding, and I know where I can put my hands on a nifty church seal."

He held up his hands to ward me off. "I know better than to come between a woman and her sleep, her breakfast, or Dora's apple pie. I'll call you this evening."

Dora took off for home, and Ike drove my car to my house. After a few minutes of silence, I couldn't stand it.

"Go ahead, tell me what a stupid cow I am for not calling the barracks as soon as I found that disk. But I never expected a murderer to show up in broad daylight."

"Dawn doesn't qualify as broad daylight," he said. "*Stupid cow*? Where does that come from?"

"Tom Martin called me that when he was trying to get me to type a suicide note."

"Ouch. I'll bet that bothered you as much as having a gun at your head."

"Not by half. All the nasty names in the world won't spray my brains over the office."

"Yuck. Gross." He made gagging sounds as he stopped the car in Dora's driveway.

"Yuck? Where's my tough cop?" I said.

Without answering, he got out, walked around the car, opened my door, and pulled me out of the seat and against him. "Your tough cop is right here, awfully glad you're in one piece."

His kiss tasted of peppermint and coffee. "In one piece for now," I admitted. "I feel as if I might need someone to glue me back together any minute."

"I'll bring my duct tape."

Dora opened her front door. "Hurry up, Abby. The eggs are getting cold."

"I'll see you tomorrow," Ike said. "And I'll phone tonight. You call me if you need me before that."

I smiled and waved, then ran up the walk toward ham and eggs and toast and a warm old quilt tucked around me so I could sleep. If I could get my mind to turn off its pictures of this morning and of the impending visit from the bishop.

Chapter Eighteen

On the third ring I snatched the phone from its cradle and turned off my computer. The eighth and final draft of my homily for that night's Christmas Eve service lay in all its printed glory in front of me, and a warm feeling hugged my heart.

When I recognized my mother's voice, my inner temperature fell.

"Abigail," she said, "I have such good news."

"Merry Christmas, Mom. Tell me your news."

"Oh, save your holiday greetings. You're going to give them to us right here, at your own home." Her excitement depressed me. I knew I would shortly displease her.

"No, Mom. I told you I can't fly out there. I have too much work, I haven't asked the church for any time off, and I couldn't get a ticket now, in any case." I scrunched my eyelids to keep from rolling my eyes. Even over the phone, my mother could hear eyes rolling from hundreds of miles away.

"Don't roll your eyes, young lady. You haven't heard the wonderful deal I worked out. Right there in Frederick I found this terrific travel agent. She can get you on a plane out of Dulles International late tomorrow morning that will put you at home in time for Christmas dinner."

I bit my lip and swallowed a scream. "What a great

thought, Mom. However, I can't visit you this holiday. I already told you that."

"You told me all the obstacles to coming home. I've removed them. You don't have to worry about the cost. Wait till you see the tickets. You won't believe the price I got." I could hear my mother's beads clinking as she paced. "And I booked your return flight for Saturday morning, so you'll be back in plenty of time for your Sunday service."

"Mom, it's not just the cost. I'm not going to pick up the tickets."

"I realize what a busy day this is for you. That's why I'm calling so early, to get you before you leave for church. Poor thing, preaching this morning for the Fourth Sunday in Advent and then leading two services tonight for Christmas Eve. The agent said she could send the tickets out to you via courier. Do you want them to come to your house or to the church?"

"I don't want them at all. I can't make it, really. I have a sermon to write."

"Okay, spoil your surprise. I promised your father I wouldn't tell you about your present no matter what, but I can see I have to. We got you a brand new laptop. You can write the sermon here. I have club on Thursday, so that would be a good day. Then we can go over to Aunt Sarah's in the evening."

For fun, Aunt Sarah's get-togethers ranked right up there with going over a cliff in my car. Right behind having a gun held to my head. "She doesn't plan to introduce me to some eligible guy, does she? The last one was forty years old."

"Well, Miss Picky, he had his own insurance agency and looked a very young forty." Any unmarried male under ninety counted in Mom's book as a prospective husband for her hopelessly unmarried daughter. "You'll like this one. He plays tennis and just joined his father's dental practice. Beautiful teeth, and the cutest little mustache."

I shuddered. "Mom, I mean it. Forget the plane tickets. I can't come. I have plans here."

"But I already gave the travel agent my MasterCard number!"

I grabbed the receiver and squeezed. "Call her back and cancel your order."

My mother switched tones. "Your father spent days researching the best laptop to buy you. He'll be so disappointed if you don't come to open it. He says laptops are much too delicate to send through the mail. Who knows when we'll see you to give it to you? You don't want to disappoint Daddy, do you?"

If they gave Oscars for dramatic performances over the phone, my mother would have an army of those naked gold guys on her mantel.

"Please explain to Dad that I already made plans. Maryland is my home now." I hoped that would continue to be true after the bishop's visit later in the day. "I'm dating someone, and he invited me to have Christmas dinner at his mother's."

"Oh, Abby!" my mother squealed. "I'm delighted. A parishioner of yours?"

"No. I met him after the murder at my church. He's a state trooper."

"You mean a cop, a common cop."

"I don't think state police officers would consider themselves common. He's funny, bright, and my age."

"I noticed you didn't mention his looks."

"My neighbor Dora calls him Officer Hunk. That should give you some idea."

"That woman is coarser than lye soap. If she approves of him, I hate to think what he's like."

"We've only dated a few times. Our relationship hasn't advanced to the stage where I'm ready for you to meet him." Nor had I given Ike anything like the warning he was entitled to before he met my parents.

"A cop, Abby. Cops make terrible husbands. They drink. They have a divorce rate multiple times the national average. Maybe one out of a hundred qualifies as something better than a sleazebag with a badge. If you'd only come home and meet Aunt Sarah's dentist's son."

"Sorry, Mom, no can do. Kisses and hugs. Have to run. Time to get ready for church."

"You're truly not coming home."

"I am home. Here. I'm not coming to your home this Christmas. I'll come visit sometime in the new year." Or the one after that. Unless I got fired and had nowhere to sleep.

"I suppose I'll have to call that travel agent. She might not agree to cancel the tickets. Then I'm stuck for the price."

"Talk tough, Mom. You can bring her around to your point of view." The State Department should send my mother to the Middle East. She could talk the Palestinians and the Israelis into an agreement.

On second thought, she might aggravate them so badly no peace talks would occur for the rest of the century.

"Daddy's going to be upset to hear you're not coming after all."

"Give him my love. Have a happy holiday. Goodbye, Mom." I hung up and went on a hunt for the strongest headache medicine in the house.

The family service of lessons and carols proceeded with only one hitch, a shepherd who insisted on hooking one of the angel's wings and pulling them off her shoulders. She gave him a discreet swat on the back of his head, and he straightened up like a good worshipper at the manger. I knew the bishop had to be sitting out there somewhere, but I couldn't locate him. Maybe he hadn't made it in time.

No such luck. After the final hymn, Alvin approached me as I shook hands with the people going out the front door. "He's here, and we're meeting in the usual place." He gave me a triumphant smirk.

When I took the last seat around the table, Alvin stroked his tie as if urging those blasted ferocious Santas to whip their reindeer mounts to a final victory. He cleared his throat. "Bishop, shouldn't we ask Pastor Shaw to wait in her office while we discuss these matters?"

The bishop gave Alvin a long and irritated look. "That was your first mistake, Mr. Porter. When you attempted to exclude Pastor Shaw from your board meeting, you violated not only your congregation's constitution, but the rules of our national body as well."

First mistake? I began to believe I might enjoy this meeting.

The bishop reached into his briefcase and pulled out a plump leather portfolio. "Since we talked, Mr. Porter, I made some calls to the other board members, to individuals they suggested, and to people with a history of service to the larger church. Discounting the report of your member subsequently arrested for the murder of St. Luke's altar guild president, the data in here is amazingly one-sided."

"You can't go by the sympathy vote," Alvin whined. "Yes, she had a terrible experience, but that doesn't make her a good pastor."

"The witness of the people of this congregation," the bishop continued, "presents a picture of a concerned, hard-working, compassionate minister. Someone admired and trusted by the members of St. Luke's. Someone they would not wish to see removed from office."

"It's the holiday spirit," Alvin insisted. "No one wants to say anything bad about the pastor during the Christmas season. And they're taking on the blame because of Tom. You didn't get a realistic picture. After the holidays are over, people will wake up. They'll realize they don't want a pastor who's tainted with connection to a murder, who ran around out-investigating the police instead of doing her

job. Call them back in late January. I move we continue
studying Pastor Shaw's fitness for ministry."

The bishop shook his head. "You don't understand, Mr.
Porter. The matter is settled. I've scrutinized your accusations, the parishioners' attitudes, and the pastor's record. I
see no grounds for continuing this probe. Will the secretary
please record that I have pronounced my judgment? I ab-
solve Pastor Abigail Shaw of all the allegations against her,
I commend her for her fine work of ministry, and I exhort
the people of St. Luke's to support her in every way possible."

He handed each board member a copy of a letter sum-
marizing his declaration and gave the original to the secretary for entry into the congregation's records. Alvin sat
stunned and defeated, apparently unable to move and un-
willing to accept the end of his crusade.

"Please stay a moment, Pastor Shaw," the bishop re-
quested. "You, too, Mr. Porter. I have some things to say
to each of you that I'd like the other to hear."

My heart sank. I'd thought I was out of the woods. A
tiny smile flitted around Alvin's mouth. He'd caught my
discomfort and thought he might yet get a part of what he
wanted.

"My secretary promised I'd get back to you before tonight, Pastor Shaw. Because of seasonal activities and
spending a longer period than expected researching the situation at St. Luke's, I didn't."

He opened his daybook and checked his records. "I
called one morning, but I believe that was the day of your
unfortunate encounter with Judge Martin. My apologies.
You've won my respect for the manner in which you've
handled all of this, from a murder in your church and the
subsequent disruption to your grace under fire during a vicious and unwarranted personal attack."

"Well," Alvin grumbled, "I may have been direct and
even a little rough, but when you say unwarranted—"

"You have had your chance to speak, Mr. Porter." The bishop raised his voice, which lost its gentle tone. "Now you have a chance to listen, and I suggest you do so carefully. You have acted with malice. Not only do you owe your pastor an apology, you should consider whether being on the board produces an undue pressure on you."

Alvin turned paler than his eggshell shirt. "You're saying I should resign."

The bishop smiled. "You should at the very least give the matter prayerful consideration. If you discover you cannot wholeheartedly support Pastor Shaw in her leadership of St. Luke's, then you owe it to the parish and your own health not to put yourself in the kind of position you're in tonight."

Now Alvin's color reversed itself, and he began to resemble the scarlet paraments we use only during Holy Week. He struggled to rise, as if his legs wouldn't obey him.

"Please stay seated," the bishop said. "I have just a little more to say. Again with prayerful deliberation and an honest look at your own life and mind, you should ask yourself whether you would be happier in another church."

Alvin's jaw dropped, but nothing came out. I thought of the speechless boy in the pageant the week before.

"You may go now." The bishop's voice had regained its gentleness, but the dismissal came through clearly.

Alvin rasped, "Merry Christmas, Bishop. Merry Christmas, Pastor." He stumbled from the room looking ten years older than he had when I sat down. In spite of the agony he'd caused me, my heart went out to him.

The bishop lay his hand on mine. "I can see your sympathy for this man. Give him a few days or weeks to decide what's important to him, the glory of the battle or the chance to start over. If you approach him now, he'll think you're gloating."

"What do I have to gloat over?" I asked.

"Actually," he replied, "quite a lot." He tilted his head and gazed at me over his glasses, inviting me to acknowledge my victories.

I nodded. "Yes. Or at least to be thankful for."

"I have to be back in Baltimore for a midnight service. I wish you every joy of the season and continued success in your ministry here at St. Luke's."

Then, to my amazement, he hugged me. "Way to go, Abby," he said. "Most of our best ministers are survivors of some sort."

The whole congregation seemed to soar through the late Christmas Eve service. Warren's playing reached new heights. He blended old hymns only classical music buffs would recognize with familiar tunes and brought satisfied smiles to everyone's lips.

During my homily, I mentioned both the church's ordeal and my own as a result of Nancy's murder. I paralleled our escape into tonight's joy of the season to God's intention in taking on human form to be with us in all our struggles.

Not one line of the choir's anthems went flat. Not a single person stormed off angry because they'd received a wilted poinsettia after paying as much as the people who got the healthy ones. Not one candle tilted far enough to overheat its glass globe and explode.

After I'd shaken all the parishioners' hands and wished them a joyful holiday, I made my way to the sacristy, not sure whether I was walking or floating. Warren stopped me just short of my goal.

"You found it," I said. "Marvelous music, absolutely magical."

"Actually," he replied, "I never did locate the thing. I decided if you could improvise well enough with the church seal to vanquish a murderer, I could do the same to a few hymns with a mighty pipe organ."

I stepped into the sacristy with relief. Then I hung up my robes in a hurry, anxious to get home.

The door swung open, and a small woman I'd never seen gazed around the room. "So this is where it happened," she said.

"Yes, Nancy Huff was murdered in this room," I replied.

"Oh, I suppose so. But I meant you met my son here."

Ike stepped through the doorway. "We got here a little late, so I had to park the car halfway to Thurmont. It's in front of the church now, Mom, all ready for you."

She gifted me with a smile full of generosity and kindness. "Don't forget that dinner's at one o'clock sharp. The menfolk get grumpy if you make them wait too long for their food." She winked and started out the door.

"Ike," she said in a stage whisper, "I don't have any idea what kind of a date she is, but she's one dynamite preacher." I heard the click of her heels get fainter as she proceeded toward the car.

We stood together awkwardly. Then he took my hand and kissed it. "She's right. You are dynamite."

"As a preacher," I said.

He grinned in the way that threatened to melt my fillings. "That, too."

I hugged him with abandon. "St. Luke's and I have had an awful Advent, but somehow I know Christmas and the new year will make up for it."